D0724605

"I look upon Sturgeon with a secret and growing jealousy." —Ray Bradbury.

"One of the greats in the field."
—*Publishers Weekly*

Also by Theodore Sturgeon published by
Carroll & Graf:

The Dreaming Jewels

Venus Plus X

THEODORE
STURGEON
Venus Plus X

DISCARDED
JENKS LRC
GORDON COLLEGE

JENKS L.R.C.
GORDON COLLEGE
255 GRAPEVINE RD.
WENHAM, MA 01984-1895

Carroll & Graf Publishers, Inc.
New York

P.S
3569
.T875
V 4
1988

Copyright © 1960 by Theodore Sturgeon
Copyright © renewed 1987 by the Estate of Theodore Sturgeon

All rights reserved

Reprinted by arrangement with Bluejay Books, Inc

First Carroll & Graf edition 1988

Carroll & Graf Publishers, Inc.
260 Fifth Avenue
New York, NY 10001

ISBN: 0-88184-387-3

Manufactured in the United States of America

Venus Plus X

"*Charlie Johns*," urgently cried Charlie Johns: "*Charlie Johns, Charlie Johns!*" for that was the absolute necessity—to know who Charlie Johns was, not to let go of that for a second, for anything, ever.

"I *am* Charlie Johns," he said argumentatively, and plaintively, he said it again. No one argued, no one denied it. He lay in the warm dark with his knees drawn up and his arms crossed and his forehead pressed tight against his kneecaps. He saw dull flickering red, but that was inside his eyelids, and he was Charlie Johns.

C. *Johns* once stencilled on a foot-locker, written in speedball black-letter on a high-school diploma, typed on a paycheck. *Johns, Chas.* in the telephone book.

The name, all right. All right, fine, okay, but a man is more than a name. A man is twenty-seven years old, he sees the hairline just so in his morning mirror and likes a drop of Tabasco on his eggs (over light: whites firm, yolks runny). He was born with one malformed toe and a strabismus. He can cook a steak drive a car love a girl run a mimeograph go to the bathroom brush his teeth, including the permanent bridge, left upper lateral incisor and bicuspid. He left the house in plenty of time but he is going to be late to work.

He opened his eyes and it wasn't dull flickering red at all, but grey—a cold sourceless silver, grey like snail trails on the lilac leaves—a springtime thing, that. Spring it was, oh that springtime thing; it was love last night, Laura, she—

When daylight saving time is new, the daylit evening is forever, and you can do so much. How he *begged* Laura for the chance to get her screens up; if Mom could have seen that, now! And down in Laura's stinking cellar, shuffling through the half-dark with the screens under his arm, he had walked into the cruel point of the dangling strap-hinge of a discarded shutter, torn a hole in his brown tweed pants, punched a red blood-bruise (with warp and woof stamped on it) on his thigh. And worth it, worth it, all that forever-evening, with a girl, a real girl (she could prove it) for all the long end of the evening; and all the way home love! of here and of now, and spring of course, and oh of course *love!* said the tree-frogs, the lilacs, the air, and the way sweat dried on him. (Good—this is good. Good to be a part of here and of now, and spring of course, and oh of course, love; but best of all, to remember, to know it all, Charlie.) Better than love just to remember home, the walk between high hedges, the two white lamps with the big black 61 painted on each (Mom had done that for the landlord; she was clever with her hands) only they were pretty weathered by now, yes the hands too. The foyer with the mottled brass wall-full of mailboxes and discreet pushbuttons for the tenants, and the grille of the house phone that had never worked since they moved here, and that massive brass plate solidly concealing the electric lock, which for years he had opened with a blow of his shoulder, never breaking stride . . . and get closer, closer, because it is so important to remember; nothing remembered is important; it's remembering that matters; you can! you can!

The steps from the ground floor had old-fashioned nickel-plated nosings over carpet worn down to the backing, red fuzz at the edges. (Miss Mundorf taught first grade, Miss Willard taught second grade, Miss Hooper taught fifth. Remember *everything*.) He looked around him, where he lay remembering in the silver light; the soft walls were unlike metal and unlike fabric but rather like both, and it was very warm . . . he went on remembering with his eyes open: the flight from the second floor to the third had the nickel nosing too, but no carpeting, and the steps were all hollowed, oh, very slightly; mounting them, you could be thinking about anything, but that clack clack, as a change from the first flight's flap flap, put you right there, you knew where you were . . .

Charlie Johns screamed, "Oh God—*where am I?*"

He unfolded himself, rolled over on his stomach, drew up his knees, and then for a moment could move no more. His mouth was dry and hot inside as pillowslips creasing under Mom's iron; his muscles, leg and back, all soft and tight-tangled like the knitting basket Mom was going to clean out some day . . .

. . . love with Laura, spring, the lights with 61, the shoulder on the lock, up the stairs flap flap, clack clack and—surely he could remember the rest of the way, because he had gone in gone to bed gotten up left for work . . . hadn't he? Hadn't he?

Shakily he pressed himself up, knelt, weakly squatted. His head dropped forward and he rested, panting. He watched the brown fabric of his clothes as if it were a curtain, about to open upon unknown but certain horror.

And it did.

"The brown suit," he whispered. Because there on his thigh was the little rip (and under it the small hurtful bulge of the checkered bruise) to prove that he had not dressed for work this morning, had not even reached the top of the second flight. Instead, he was—here.

Because he could not stand just yet, he hunched around, fists and knees, blinking and turning his unsteady head. Once he stopped and touched his chin. It had no more stubble than it should have for a man coming home from a date he had shaved for.

He turned again and saw a tall oval finely scribed into the curved wall. It was the first feature he had been able to discover in this padded place. He gaped at it and it gave him Nothing.

He wondered what time it was. He lifted his arm and turned his head and got his ear to his watch. It was, thank God, still running. He looked at it. He looked at it for a long time without moving. He seemed not to be able to read it. At last he was able to understand that the numerals were the wrong way round, mirror-reversed; 2 was where 10 should be, 8 where four should be. The hands pointed to what should have been eleven minutes to eleven, but was, if this watch really were running backwards, eleven minutes past one. And it was running backwards. The sweep second-hand said so.

And do you know, Charlie, something under the terror and the wonderment said to him, do you know, all you want to do, even now, is remember? there was the terrible old battleax you got for Algebra 3 in high school, when you'd flunked Algebra 1 and had to take it over, and had gone through Algebra 2 and Geometry 1 on your belly, and flunked Geometry 2 and had to take it over—remember? and then for Algebra 3 you got this Miss Moran, and she was like IBM, with teeth. And then one day you asked her about something that puzzled you a little and the way she answered, you had to ask more . . . and she opened a door for you that you never knew was there, and she herself became something . . . well, after that, you watched her and knew what the frozen mien, the sharp discipline, the sheer inhumanity of the woman was for. She was just waiting for someone to come and ask her questions about mathematics a little beyond, a little outside the book. And it was as if she had long ago despaired of finding anyone that would. Why it meant so much to her was that she loved mathematics in a way that made it a pity the word "love" had ever been used for anything else. And also that from minute to minute she never knew if some kid asking questions would be the last she'd ever know, or open a door for, because she was dying of cancer, which nobody never even suspected until she just didn't show up one day.

Charlie Johns looked at the faint oval in the soft silver wall and wished Miss Moran could be here. He also wished Laura could be here. He could remember them both so clearly, yet they were so many years apart from each other (and how many, he thought, looking at his wrist watch, how many years from me?) He wished Mom could be here, and the Texas redhead. (She was the first time for him, the redhead; and how would she mix with Mom? For that matter, how would Laura mix with Miss Moran?)

He could not stop remembering; dared not, and did not want to stop. Because as long as he kept remembering, he knew he was

Charlie Johns; and although he might be in a new place without knowing what time it was, he wasn't lost, no one is ever lost, as long as he knows who he is.

Whimpering with effort, he got to his feet. He was so weak and muzzy-headed that he could only stand by bracing his feet wide apart; he could only walk by flailing his arms to keep his balance. He aimed for the faint oval line on the wall because it was the only thing here to aim for, but when he tried to go forward he progressed diagonally sidewise; it was like the time (he remembered) at the fun house at Coney Island, where they get you in a room and close it up and unbeknownst to you they tilt it a little to one side, you with no outside reference; and only green mirrors to see yourself in. They used to have to hose it out five, six times a day. He felt the same way now; but he had an advantage; he knew who he was, and in addition he knew he was sick. As he stumbled on the soft curved part where the floor became wall, and sank on one knee on the resilient silver, he croaked, "I'm not myself just now, that's all." Then he heard his own words properly and leapt to his feet: "Yes I am!" he shouted, "I am!"

He tottered forward, and since there was nothing to hold on the oval—it was only a thin line, taller than he was—he pushed against it.

It opened.

There was someone waiting outside, smiling, dressed in such a way that Charlie gasped and said, "Oh, I beg your pardon . . ." and then pitched forward on his face.

Herb Raile lives out in Homewood, where he has a hundred and fifty feet on Begonia Drive, and two hundred and thirty feet back to where Smitty Smith's begins its two-hundred-and-thirty-foot run to its one-hundred-fifty-foot frontage on Calla Drive. Herb Raile's house is a split-level, Smith's a rancher. Herb's neighbors to the right and left have splits.

Herb wheels into the drive and honks and puts his head out. "Surprise!"

Jeanette is mowing the lawn with a power mower and with all that racket, the car horn makes her jump immoderately. She puts her foot on the grounding-plate and holds it down until the mower stops, and then runs laughing to the car.

"Daddy, Daddy!"

"Daddy, daddy, dad*eee!*" Davy is five, Karen three.

"Oh, honey, why are you *home!*"

"Closed the Arcadia account, and the great man says, Herb, he says, go on home to your kids. You look cool." Jeanette is in shorts and a T-shirt.

"I was a good boy, I was a good boy," Davy shrills, poking in Herb's side pocket.

"I was a good boy too," shrieks Karen.

Herb laughs and scoops her up. "Oh, what a man you'll grow up to be!"

"Shush, Herb, you'll get her all mixed up. Did you remember the cake?"

Herb puts down the three-year-old and turns to the car. "Cake *mix*. Much better when you bake it yourself." Stilling her moan, he adds, "I'll do it, I'll do it. I can slam up a better cake than you any old day. Butter, toilet paper."

"Cheese?"

"Damn. I got talking to Louie." He takes the parcel and goes in to change. While he is gone, Davy puts his foot where Jeanette put her foot when she stopped the mower. The cylinder head is still hot. Davy is barefoot. When Herb comes out again Jeanette is saying, "Shh. Shh. Be a man."

Herb is wearing shorts and a T-shirt.

*I*t wasn't maidenly modesty that made Charlie Johns keel over like that. Anything could have done it—a flashlight in the face, the sudden apparition of steps going down. And anyway, he'd thought it was a woman dressed like that. He hadn't been able to think of anyone else but women since he found himself in that tank— Laura, Mom, Miss Moran, the Texas redhead. He could see why a flash glance at this character would make anyone think so. Not that he could really see anything at the moment; he was lying flat on his back on something resilient but not so soft as the tank— rather like those wheel tables they have in hospitals. And someone was gently working on a cut high on his forehead, while a cool wet cloth smelling remotely like witch hazel lay blissfully across the rest of his forehead and his eyes. But whoever it was was talking to him, and though he couldn't understand a word, he didn't think it was a woman's voice. It was no *basso profundo,* but it wasn't a woman's voice. Oh brother, what a get-up. Imagine a sort of short bathrobe, deep scarlet, belted, but opening sharply away above and below. Above it was cut back behind the arms, and back of the neck a stiff collar stood up higher than the top of the head; it was shaped like the back of an upholstered chair and was darn near as big. Below the belt the garment cut back and down just as sharply to come together in a swallow-tail like a formal coat. In front, under the belt, was a short silky arrangement something like what the Scot wears in front of his kilt and calls a sporran. Very soft-looking slipper-socks, the same color as the robe, and with sharp-cut, floppy points front and back, came up to about mid-calf.

Whatever the treatment was, it killed the throb in his forehead with almost shocking suddenness. He lay still a moment, afraid that it might rear up and bash him as suddenly, but it didn't. He put up a tentative hand, whereupon the cloth was snatched away from his eyes and he found himself looking up into a smiling face which said several fluid syllables, ending in an interrogative trill.

Charlie said, "Where am I?"

The face shrugged its eyebrows and laughed pleasantly. Firm cool fingers touched his lips, and the head wagged from side to side.

Charlie understood, so said, "I don't understand you either." He reared up on one elbow and looked around him. He felt much stronger.

He was in a large, stubbily T-shaped chamber. Most of the stem of the T was taken up by the—call it padded cell he had left; its door stood open still. Inside and out, it gleamed with that sourceless, soft, cold silver light. It looked like a huge pumpkin with wings.

The whole top of the T, floor to ceiling and from end to end, was a single transparent pane. Charlie thought he might have seen one as large in a department-store show-window, but he doubted it. At each end of the T were drapes; he presumed there were doors there.

Outside it was breathtaking. A golf-course can sometimes present rolling green something like that—but not miles, square miles of it. There were stands of trees here and there, and they were tropical; the unmistakable radiance of the *flamboyante* could be seen, nearly felt, it was so vivid; and there were palms—traveler's, cabbage, and coconut palms, and palmettos; tree-ferns and flowering cacti. On a clump of stone ruins, so very picturesque they might almost have been built there for the purpose of being picturesque ruins, stood a magnificent strangler fig nearly a hundred feet high, with its long clutching roots and multiple trunks matching the arch and droop of its glossy foliage.

The only building to be seen—and they were up quite high—

twelve or fourteen stories, Charlie guessed, and on high ground at that—was impossible.

Take a cone—a dunce cap. Taper it about three times as tall as it ought to be. Now bend it into a graceful curve, almost to a quarter circle. Now invert it, place its delicate tip in the ground and walk away, leaving its heavy base curving up and over and supported by nothing at all. Now make the whole thing about four hundred feet high, with jewel-like groups of pleasantly asymmetrical windows, and oddly placed, curved balconies which seemed to be of, rather than on, the surface, and you have an idea of that building, that impossible building.

Charlie Johns looked at it, and at his companion, and, open-mouthed, at the building and back again. The man looked, and did not look human. The eyes were almost too far apart and too long—a little more of both, and they'd have been on the sides rather than the front of his face. The chin was strong and smooth, the teeth prominent and excellent, the nose large and with nostrils so high-arched that only a fraction of arc spared them from belonging to some horse. Charlie already knew that those fingers were strong and gentle; so was the face, the whole mien and carriage. The torso was rather longer, somehow, than it ought to be, the legs a little shorter than, if Charlie were an artist, he would have drawn them. And of course, those clothes . . .

"I'm on Mars," quavered Charlie Johns, meaning to be funny somehow, and sounding pitiably frightened. He made a useless gesture at the building.

To his surprise, the man nodded eagerly and smiled. He had a warm and confident smile. He pointed to Charlie, to himself, and to the building, took a step toward the enormous window and beckoned.

Well, why not? . . . yet Charlie cast a lingering glance back at the door of the silver cell from which he had emerged. Little as he liked it, it was the only thing here which was remotely familiar to him.

The man sensed his feeling, and made a reassuring, sort of U-turn gesture toward the distant building and back to the cell.

With a half-hearted smile, Charlie agreed to go.

The man took him briskly by the arm and marched off, not to the draped ends of the room, but straight to the window, straight *through* the window. This last he did by himself. Charlie dug in his heels and fled back to the wheeled table.

The man stood outside, firmly on thin air, and beckoned, smiling. He called to Charlie too, but Charlie only saw that; there was no sound. When one is in an enclosed place, one feels it—actually, one hears it—in any case, one knows it, and Charlie *knew* it. Yet that bright-robed creature had stepped through whatever enclosed it, leaving it enclosed, and was now impatiently, though cheerfully, calling to Charlie to join him.

There is a time for pride, thought Charlie, and this is it, and I haven't got any. He crept to the window, got down on his hands and knees, and slowly reached toward the pane. It *was* there, to ear, to spatial feel, but not to his hand. He inched outward.

The man, laughing (but laughing *with,* not laughing *at,* Charlie was certain) walked outdoors on nothing and came to him. When he made as if to take Charlie's hand, Charlie snatched it back. The man laughed again, bent and slapped hard against the level which unaccountably carried his feet. Then he stood up and stamped.

Well, obviously he was standing on *something*. Charlie, remembering (again) remembered seeing an old West Indian woman at San Juan airport, coming for no one knows what reason off her first flight, meeting her first escalator. She backed and filled and touched and jumped, until finally the husky young man with her picked her up bodily and plunked her on it. She grasped the rail and shrieked all the way up, and at the top, continued her shrieks; they were, they had been all along, shrieks of laughter.

Well, crawl he might, but he wouldn't shriek. Pale and hollow-eyed, he put a hand through where the pane wasn't, and slapped where the man had slapped.

This one he could feel.

Crawling on one hand and two knees, paddling ahead of him with the other hand, eyes slitted and head back so he would see out but not down, he passed through the nothing-at-all which so adequately enclosed the room, out upon the nothing-at-all which waited outside.

The man, whose voice he could suddenly hear again, laughingly beckoned him farther out, but Charlie was as far out as he intended to be. So to his horror the man suddenly swooped on him, lifted him bodily, and bumped his right hand down on a midair nothing about waist high to him—a handrail!

Charlie gazed at his right hand, apparently empty but grasping a blessed something; he could see the flattened flesh at the side of his grip, the whitening knuckles. He placed his other hand beside it and looked across the breeze—there was quite a breeze—at the other, who said something in his singing tongue and pointed downward. Reflexively Charlie Johns looked down, and gasped. It was probably no more than two hundred feet, but they looked to him like miles. He gulped and nodded, for obviously the man had said something cheerful like "Helluva drop, hey?" Too late, he realized that the man had said the equivalent of, "Shall we, old boy?" and he had gone and nodded his head.

They dropped. Charlie shrieked. It was not laughter.

THE BON TON ALLEYS ARE—IS—A COMPLEX, CONSISTING OF, NATurally, bowling alleys, and of course an adjoining bar; but a good deal has been added. To the tissue-dispensers, for example, a second teensy-weensy dispenser for teensy tissues for milady's lipstick. To the bar, as well, foamy cottage curtains and a floor-length skirt around the pretzel-and-egg stand. The barmaid has become somehow a waitress. No one has traced the evolution from beer out of cans to pink ladies and even excuse-the-expression vermouth and soda. The pool tables are gone and are replaced by a gifte shoppe.

Here sit Jeanette Raile and her neighbor, Tillie Smith, over a well-earned (Tillie, especially, is getting to be a first-line, league-type bowler) crème de menthe frappé, and get down to the real business of the evening, which is—business.

"Accounting is accounting," says Jeanette, "and copy is copy. So why does old Beerbelly keep throwing his weight around in the copy department?"

Tillie sips and delicately licks. "Seniority," she says, a word which explains so much. Her husband works in the public relations department of Cavalier Industries.

Jeanette frowns. Her husband works for the agency that has the Cavalier account. "He can't push *us* around."

"Oh," yawns Tillie, whose husband is a little older and doubtless, in some ways, a good deal sharper than Herb, "those adding-machine people are easy to handle, because they're so awfully good at seeing what's in front of them."

"What could be not in front of them?"

"Like that old Trizer that used to be with Cavalier," Tillie said. "One of the boys—now don't ask me which one—wanted a little more room in the office, so he had a chat with the Great Man—you know, funny funny—and made a bar-bet sort of thing that he could pad the old expense account right through the ceiling and old Trizer would never catch it." She sips, she laughs lightly.

"What happened?" asks Jeanette, agog.

"Why, old Trizer knew my—uh, this boy was after him, so when the heavy swindle-sheets started coming in, he quietly began to collect them until he had a stack heavy enough to drop on this boy's head. But the boy fed them out so carefully that it took a while. Meanwhile, of course, the Great Man was getting copies each time he did it, just to keep the funny funny gag alive. So by the time Trizer had his bomb ready to drop, five weeks had gone by and that was too long for the Great Man to think it was funny anymore. So now they kicked old Trizer upstairs to the rear ranks of the Board of Directors where his seniority can't hurt anyone but himself."

"Just deserts," says Jeanette.

Tillie laughs. "Sounds like a good name for a high-class bakery."

"Just Desserts . . . Oh yes," says Jeanette brightly, for she hadn't thought of it until now, "Herb's using that line to head up a new presentation to snag the Big-Bug Bakeries account. Be a dear and don't tell anyone." Meanwhile she will tell Herb, but with the grasshopper speech—jump, boy, jump.

*T*hey stood on springy turf, *Charlie with buckled knees, his* companion's arm around him, holding him up. Charlie shook himself and stood, and when he could, he looked up. He then shuddered so hard that the arm tightened around him. He made an immense effort and grinned and threw off the arm. His companion made a small speech, with gestures for up, for down, for fast, for the bump on Charlie's head, for a matrix of humilities which probably included "I'm sorry." Charlie grinned again and feebly clapped him on the back. He then cast another worried look upward and moved away from the building. Not only was it altogether too big, much too high; the bulk of it seemed to be hanging over him like a fist. It was as wild a piece of architecture as the other, though more spindle-shaped than conical, more topple than top.

They moved across the turf—there seemed to be no roads or paths—and if Charlie had thought his companion's odd garb might attract attention, he was disabused. He himself was much more of an oddment. Not that the people peered, or crowded about: by no means. But one could sense by their cheerful waves and quickly averted eyes that they were curious, and further, that curiosity was out of place.

Rounding the building, they came upon perhaps fifty of them splashing in the pool. For bathing suits they wore only the soft silky sporran things, which clung to them without visible means of support; but by this time this was a category he was prepared to accept. They were, without exception, gravely polite in greeting him with a wave, a smile, a word, and apparently happy to see his companion.

Away from the pool, they wore a great many kinds and styles of clothes—often two by two, though he failed to catch the significance, if any, of this. It might be as little as a vivid, all but fluorescent ribbon of orange about the biceps—plus, of course, the sporran—or it might be as much as baggy pantaloons, tremendous winglike collars, steeple hats, platform sandals—there was no end to them, and, except for the ones who walked in pairs, there was no similarity between any of them except in the beauty of their colors and the richness and variety of the fabrics. Costume was obviously adornment to them, nothing more; unlike any people he had ever encountered or read about, they seemed to have no preoccupation with any particular part of their bodies.

He saw no women.

A strange place. The air was peculiarly invigorating, and the sky, though bright—with, now that he looked at it, a touch of that silvery radiance he had seen in the "padded cell"—was overcast. Flowers grew profusely, some with heady, spicy scents, many quite new to him, with color splashed on with a free and riotous hand. The turf was as impossible as the buildings—even and springy everywhere, completely without bald patches or unwanted weeds, and in just as good shape here, near the buildings, where scores of people milled about, as it was far off.

He was led around the building and through an archway which leaned inexplicably but pleasantly to the left, and his companion took him solicitously by the arm. Before he could wonder why, they dropped straight down about sixty feet, and found themselves standing in an area vaguely like a subway station, except that instead of waiting for a train they stepped—rather, the native stepped; Charlie was hauled—off the edge of the platform and had to go through the unpleasant experience of flexing his legs to take a drop that just wasn't a drop—for the pit was bridged from side to side by the invisible substance which had levitated them down the building.

Halfway across, they stopped, the man gave Charlie a querying look, Charlie braced himself for anything at all and nodded; and, just how, Charlie couldn't see—it seemed to be some sort of gesture—they were flying through a tunnel. They stood still, and there was little sensation of starting or stopping; whatever it was they stood on whisked them away at some altogether unlikely speed until, in a very few minutes, they were stopped again at another platform. They walked into a sort of square cave at the side and were flicked up to ground level under the conical building. They walked away from the subway while Charlie concentrated on swallowing his heart and decided to let his stomach follow them whenever it had a mind to.

They crossed to what appeared to be a cave-like central court, all around the walls of which the natives were flashing up, flashing down, on their invisible elevators; they were a pretty sight with their bright clothes fluttering. And the air was filled with music; he thought at first it was some sort of public address system, but found that they *sang;* softly, moving from place to place, into the public hall and out of it, in beautiful harmonies, they hummed and trilled.

Then, just as they approached a side wall, he saw something that so dumfounded him he barely noticed the experience of being flipped two hundred feet up like a squirted fruit-seed; he stood numb with astonishment, letting himself be pushed here, led there, while his whole sense of values somersaulted.

Two of the men who strolled past him in the central court were pregnant. There was no mistaking it.

He looked askance at his smiling companion—the strong face, the well-muscled arms and sturdy legs . . . true, the chin was very smooth, and—uh—he had very prominent pectoral muscles. The areola was considerably larger than those on a man . . . on the other hand, why not? The eyes were slightly different, too. What's so . . . now let's see. If "he" were a woman, then they were all women. Then where were the men?

He recalled the way sh— h— the way he had been plucked up on the first lift, in those arms, like a sack of soda crackers. Well, if that's what the women could do—what could the men do?

First he pictured giants—real twelve, fifteen-foot behemoths.

Then he pictured some puny little drone chained up in a—a service station some place in the subbasement . . .

And then he began to worry about himself. "Where are you taking me?" he demanded.

His guide nodded and smiled and took him by the forearm, and he had the choice of walking or falling flat on his face.

They came to a room.

The door opened . . . dilated, rather; it was an oval door, and it split down the middle and drew open with a snap as they approached it, and it snapped enthusiastically closed behind them.

He stopped and backed up to the door. He was permitted to. The door felt solid enough for ten like him, and not even a knob.

He looked up.

They all looked back at him.

Herb Raile goes over to see Smitty. The kids are asleep. He has an electronic baby-sitter about the size of a portable radio. He knocks, and Smitty lets him in.

"Hi."

"Hi."

He crosses to the sideboard in the dining area of Smitty's living room, puts down the sitter and plugs it in. "Whatch' doin'?"

Smitty scoops up the baby he had put on the couch when he went to answer the door. He hangs it on his shoulder where it attaches itself like a lapel. "Oh," he says, "Just generally mindin' the shop till the boss gets back."

"Boss hell," says Herb.

"You the boss in your house?"

"You know, you're kiddin'," says Herb, "but I'll give you a straight answer in case that was a question."

"Give me a straight answer in case."

"Our kind of people, there is no boss in the house anymore."

"Yeah, I did think things were gettin' out of hand."

"That's not what I mean, bonehead!"

"So what do you mean, headbone?" Smitty asks.

"It's a team, that's what I mean. There's a lot of yammering going on about the women taking over. They're not taking over. They're moving in."

"Interestin' thought. You're a good, good boy," he says, fatuously and with a sort of croon.

"I'm a what?"

"The baby, ya dumb bastard. He just burped."

"Le's see him. Years since I picked up a little one like that," says the father of three-year-old Karen. He takes the baby from Smith and holds it not quite at arms' length. "Dather dather dather." He flaps his tongue far out with each *th* sound. "Dather dather."

The baby's eyes get round and, held so under the armpits, its shoulders hunch up until its wet chin disappears in its bib. "Dather dather." The baby's eyes suddenly get almond-shaped, and it delivers a wide, empty smile with a dimple on the left, and a happy, aspirated buzz from the back of the throat. "Dather dather hey he's smiling," says Herb.

Smith ranges around behind Herb Raile where he can see. Impressed, "Goddam," he says. He puts his face next to Herb's. "Dather dather."

"You got to stick out your tongue far enough so he can see it move," says Herb. "Dather dather."

"Dather dather dather."

"Dather dather." The baby stops smiling and looks quickly from one to the other. "You're confusing him."

"So shut up," says the baby's father. "Dather dather dather." This so delights the baby that he crows and gets the hiccups.

"Scheiss," says Smith. "Come on in the kitchen while I get his water."

They go in the kitchen, Herb carrying the baby, and Smith gets a four-ounce bottle out of the refrigerator and drops it in an electric warmer. He takes the baby from Herb and hangs it on his shoulder again. The baby hiccups violently. He pats it. "Goddam I told Tillie I'd pick up in here."

"I'll be the boy-scout. You got your hands full." Herb takes dishes from the counter-top, scrapes them into a step-on can, stacks them in the sink. He flips on the hot water. It is all very familiar to him because this sink and his sink and the sinks in the houses to right and to left and beyond and behind all are the same kind of sink. He picks up the can of liquid detergent and looks at it, pursing his lips. "We never get this anymore."

"Whuffo?"

"Plays hell with your hands. Lano-Love, that's what we get now. Costs a little more but," he says, ending his sentence with "but."

" 'Two extra-lovely hands for two extra little pennies,' " says Smith, quoting a television commercial.

"So it's a commercial but just this once." Herb turns on the hot water, tempers it with a little cold, picks up the spray head and one by one begins hot-rinsing the dishes.

T here were four of them, besides the one that had brought him. Two were in identical clothes—a vivid green sort of belly-band, and on the hips, the pannier parts of a full panniered skirt. But without the skirt. The tallest one, directly in front of Charlie, wore a subverted bathrobe somewhat like that of Charlie's companion, but dyed a firelit orange. The fourth wore something cut on the lines of the lower half of an 1890 man's bathing suit, in electric blue.

As Charlie's startled gaze turned to each, each smiled. They were all sprawled, posed, lounging on low benches and some hummocky hassocky things which seemed to have grown up out of the floor. The tall one was seated at a kind of desk which seemed to have been built before and around him (her) after the seating. Their warm friendly smiles, and their relaxed posture, were heartening, and yet he had the transient feeling that these amenities were analogous to the hearty rituals of modern business, which might do anything to a stranger before it was done with him, but which began, "Sit down. Take off your shoes if you want—we're all buddies here. Have a cigar and don't call me mister."

One of the green ones spoke in this people's birdlike (if the bird were a dove) tones to the orange one, gesturing toward Charlie, and laughed. Like his companion's laugh, it didn't seem to have too much laugh *at* in it. Said companion now spoke up, and there was general merriment. The next thing Charlie knew, his erstwhile guide, red bathrobe and all, was hunkered down, eyes squinched closed, feeling about frantically on the floor. Then he began to crawl on his knees and one hand, poking the other fearfully ahead, and wearing on his face an excruciating mask of comic terror.

They howled.

Charlie felt his earlobes getting hot, a phenomenon which was, in him, a symptom of either anger or alcohol, and he was very sure which one it wasn't. "So let me in on the joke," he rumbled. Still laughing, they looked at him perplexedly, while Red-robe kept on with his imitation of a 20th-century man meeting his first invisible elevator.

Something snapped in Charlie Johns, who had been pushed, pulled, prodded, dropped, flung, amazed, embarrassed, and lost just exactly as much as he could stand plus a straw's weight. He punted the red-clad rump with all the education of a high-school varsity toe, and sent the creature skidding across the room on its mobile face, almost to the foot of the yellow one's big desk.

Utter silence fell.

Slowly the red-robed one got up, turned to face him, while tenderly fondling the bruised backside.

Charlie pressed his shoulders a little harder against the unyielding door and waited. One by one he met five pairs of eyes. In each was no anger, and very little surprise; just sorrow; and he found that more ominous than fury. "Well God damn it," he said to the red robe, "You asked for it!"

One of them cooed, and another chortled an answer. Then the red-robed one came forward and made a much more elaborate version of the series of moans and gestures which Charlie had seen before: the "O I'm a swine, I didn't mean to hurt your feelings" message. Charlie got it, but was vexed by it; he wanted to say, well if you feel it was so wrong, why were you stupid enough to do it?

The yellow one rose, slowly and imposingly, and somehow got disentangled from the embrace of the desk. With a warm and pitying expression, he uttered a three-syllable word and gestured behind him, where a door opened, or rather a part of the wall dilated. There was a soft ululation of assent, and they all nodded and smiled and beckoned and waved toward it.

Charlie Johns moved forward just far enough to enable him to see through the doorway. What he saw was, as he had expected, heavily loaded with the unfamiliar, but none of the svelte, oddly unbalanced, interflowing gadgetry he saw could conceal the over-all function of the flat padded table in its pool of light, the helmet-shaped business at one end, the clamp-like devices where arms and legs might go; this was some sort of operating room, and he wanted no part of it.

He stepped sharply backwards, but there were three people behind him. He whipped up a fist and found it gripped and held, high and helpless, just where it was. He tried to kick, and a bare leg flashed and locked knees with him, and it was a very strong leg indeed. The one in the orange robe came smiling apologetically and pressed a white sphere the size of a ping-pong ball against his right biceps. The ball clicked and collapsed; Charlie filled his lungs to yell but could never remember thereafter whether he had managed a sound.

"**S**EE THIS?" HERB SAYS. THEY ARE IN SMITH'S LIVING ROOM. Herb is idly turning the pages of the newspaper. Smitty is feeding the water to the baby skillfully spread out along his forearm, and says, "What?"

"Brief briefs—but for men."

"You mean underwear?"

"Like a bikini only less. Knit. My God they can't weigh more'n a quarter ounce."

"They don't. Best thing to come along since the cocktail onion."

"You got?"

"You damn bet I got. How much there?"

Herb consults the advertisement in the newspaper. "Dollar'n a half."

"You stop by Price Busters Discount over on Fifth. Two for two seventy-three."

Herb looks at the illustration. "Comes in white, black, pale yellow, pale blue and pink."

"Yup," Smitty says. Carefully he withdraws the nipple; the baby, hiccups corrected, is now asleep.

"*C*ome on, Charlie—wake up!"

Oh Mom just four more minutes I won't be late honest to pete I got in nearly two o'clock and I hope you never find out how pooped I was never mind what time. Mom?

"Charlie . . . I can't tell you how sorry I am . . ." Sorry, Laura? *But I wanted it to be perfect.* So who in real life ever makes it together the very first time? Come on, come on . . . it's easy to fix; we just do it again. . . . *Oh-h-h . . . Charlie . . .*

"Charlie?" Your name Charlie? *Just call me Red.*

. . . once when he was fourteen (he remembered, remembered), there was this girl called Ruth and there was a sort of kiss-the-pillow kid's party, and no kidding, they played post office. The post office was the kind of airlock afforded by the double outside doors and double, heavily curtained inside doors of the old-fashioned house on Sansom Street, and all during the party Charlie kept looking at Ruth. She had that special kind of warm olive skin and sleek glossy short blue-black hair. She had a crooning whispery voice and a prim mouth and shy eyes. She was afraid to look at you for more than a second, and under that olive skin you could barely see a blush but without seeing anything you knew a blush made it warmer. And when the giggling and pointing and pointless chuckling chatter led around to Charlie's name being called, and then Ruth's, so that he and she would have to go into the post office and shut the door, something in him said only, "Well, of course!" He held the door for her and she went in with her eyes cast down so they seemed closed; with her long lashes right on her warm cheeks; with her shoulders rounded with tension and her two hands hard-holding her two wrists; with her little feet making little steps; and to the yawping gallery making catcalls and kissing noises, Charlie winked broadly and then shut the door. . . . Inside she waited silently, and he was a brash and forward little rooster known for it and needing to be known for it, and he took her firmly by the shoulders. Now for the first time she uncurtained her wise shy eyes and let him fall into the far dark there, where he swam unmoving for years-long seconds; so he said, this is all I want to do with you, Ruth; and he kissed her very carefully and very lightly in the middle of her smooth hot forehead and drew back again to totter into those eyes: because, Ruth, he said, it's all I should do with you. *You understand me. Charlie*, she breathed, *you do, you do understand me*.

"You understand me, Charlie. You do, you do understand me."

He opened his eyes and fogs fled. Someone leaned close not Mom not Laura not Red not Ruth not anybody but that *thing* in the red cutaway bathrobe, who said again, "You understand me now, Charlie."

Now the words were not English, but they were as clear to him as English. He even knew the difference. The structure was different; transliterated, it would run something like "You [second person singular, but of an alternative form denoting neither intimacy nor formality, but friendship and respect, as to a beloved uncle] understand [in the simple sense of verbal, rather than emotional or psychic understanding] me [a 'me' of helpful guidance and friendliness, as from a counsellor or guide, and not that of a legal-or-other superior] Charlie." He was completely aware of all alternative words and their semantic content, although not of any cultural system which had made them that way, and he was aware that had he wanted to reply in English, he could have done so. Something had been added; nothing taken away.

He felt . . . fine. He felt as if he had done without a little sleep, and he also felt a little sheepish, from a new inner knowledge that his earlier indignation was as pointless as his fear had been; these people had not meant to ridicule him and gave no indication of wishing to harm him.

"I am Seace," said the red-robed one. "Can you understand me?"

"Sure I can!"

"Please—speak Ledom."

Charlie recognized the name—it was the term for the language, the country, and the people. Using the new tongue, he said, in wonder, "I can speak it!" He was aware that he did so with an odd accent, due probably to his physical unfamiliarity with it; like every language, it contained sounds rather more special to it than to others, like the Gaelic glottal stop, the French nasal, the Teuton guttural. Yet it was a language well designed for the ear—he had a flash recollection of his delight, when he was just a kid, of seeing a typewriter with a script type-face, and how the curly tail of each letter joined with the one following—and the Ledom syllable, aurally speaking, joined just as cleverly to the next. It filled the mouth, too, more than does modern English, just as Elizabethan English was more sonorous an instrument. It would hardly be possible to speak Ledom with the lips open and the jaw shut, as many of his contemporaries did with English, which, in its evolution, seems bound to confound the lip-reader. "I can speak it!" cried Charlie Johns, and they all cooed their congratulations; he had not felt so good about anything since the day he was seven and was cheered by all the boys on the float at a summer camp, when he swam his first strokes.

Seace took him by the upper arm and helped him to sit. They had him dressed in the almost exact equivalent of a hospital gown anywhere. He looked at this Seace (he recalled now that the "I am Seace" phrase had occurred a number of times since he "arrived," but that previously his ear had not been able to separate one phoneme from another) and he smiled, really smiled, for the first time in this strange world. This elicited another happy murmur.

Seace indicated the native in the orange garments. "Mielwis," he introduced. Mielwis stepped forward and said, "We are all very glad to have you with us."

"And this is Philos." The one in the ludicrous blue pants nodded and smiled. He had sharp humorous features, and a quick and polished glitter in his black eyes that might hide a great deal.

"And these are Nasive and Grocid," said Seace, completing the introductions.

The green-clad ones smiled their greeting, and Grocid said, "You're among friends. We want to make sure you know that, above anything else."

Mielwis, the tall one, whom the other seemed to surround with some intangible aura of respect, said, "Yes, please believe that. Trust us. And . . . if there's anything you want, just ask for it."

Harmoniously, they all chorused a ratification.

Charlie, warming toward them, wet his lips and laughed uncertainly. "Mostly, I guess . . . information is what I want."

"Anything," said Seace. "Anything at all you want to know."

"Well, then, first of all—where *am* I?"

Mielwis, waiting for the other to defer to him, said, "In the Medical One."

"This building is called the Medical One," Seace explained. "The other one, the one we came from, is the Science One."

Grocid said reverently, "Mielwis is head [the word meant 'organizer' and 'commander' and something more subtle and profound, like 'inspirer'] of the Medical One."

Mielwis smiled as if acknowledging a compliment, and said, "Seace is head of the Science One."

Seace deprecated what was apparently also a compliment, and said, "Grocid and Nasive are heads of the Children's One. You'll want to see that."

The two be-panniered ones accepted the accolade, and Grocid cooed, "I hope you will come soon."

Charlie looked from one to the other bewilderedly.

"So you see," said Seace (and the "see" was the "comprehend" expression; it was like "now you know all"), "we're all here with you."

The exact significance of this escaped Charlie, though he had the impression that it was something large—it was as if someone presented to you, at one and the same time, the Queen, the President and the Pope. He therefore said the only thing he could think of, which was, "Well, thanks . . ." which seemed to please them, and then he looked at the one unidentified person left—Philos, the one in the pants. Surprisingly, Philos winked at him. Mielwis said offhandedly, "Philos here is for you to study."

Which is not precisely what he said. The sentence was formed with a peculiar grammatical twist, somewhat like the way a man says "Onions don't like me," when he means "I don't like onions." (Or shouldn't. . . .) In any case, Philos did not seem to merit special honors and congratulations for being what he was, as did the heads of the Medical One, the Science One, and the Children's One. Maybe he just worked here.

Charlie put it away for future reference, and then looked around at their faces. They looked back attentively.

Charlie asked again, "Yes, but where *am* I?"

They looked at one another and then back at him. Seace said, "What do you mean, where are you?"

"Oh," said Seace to the others, "he wants to know *where* he is."

"Ledom," said Nasive.

"So where is Ledom?"

Again the swapped glances. Then Seace, with a the-light-is-dawning expression on his face, said, "He wants to know where Ledom is!"

"Look," said Charlie with what he thought was a reasonable amount of patience, "Let's start right from the beginning. What planet is this?"

"Earth!"

"Good. Now we—*Earth*?"

"Yes, Earth."

Charlie wagged his head. "Not any Earth I ever heard about."

Everybody looked at Philos, who shrugged and said, "That's probably so."

"It's some trick of this language," Charlie said. "If this is Earth,

I'm a . . ." He could not, in this place, with these people, think of a simile fantastic enough. "I know!" he said suddenly, "There would be a word meaning Earth—the planet I live on—in any language! I mean, the Martian word for Mars would be Earth. The Venerian word for Venus would be Earth."

"Remarkable!" said Philos.

"Nevertheless," said Mielwis, "this is Earth."

"Third planet from the sun?"

They all nodded.

"Are you and I talking about the same sun?"

"Moment to moment," murmured Philos, "nothing is ever the same."

"Don't confuse him," said Mielwis in a tone stiff as an I-beam. "Yes, it's the same sun."

"Why won't you tell me?" Charlie cried. His emotion seemed to embarrass them.

"We did. We are. We mean to," said Seace warmly. "How else can we answer? This is Earth. Your planet, ours. We were all born on it. Though at different times," he added.

"Different times? You mean . . . time travel? Is that what you're trying to tell me?"

"Time travel?" echoed Mielwis.

"We all travel in time," Philos murmured.

"When I was a kid," explained Charlie, "I used to read a lot of what we called science fiction. Do you have anything like that?"

They shook their heads.

"Stories about—well, mostly the future, but not always. Anyway, a lot of them were written about time machines—gadgets that could take you into the past or future."

They all regarded him steadily. No one said anything. He had the feeling that no one *would*. "One thing for sure," Charlie said at length, shakily, "this isn't the past" Abruptly, he was terrified. "That's it, isn't it? I'm . . . I'm in the future?"

"Remarkable!" Philos murmured.

Mielwis said gently, "We didn't think you'd come to that conclusion quite so soon."

"I t-told you," said Charlie, "I used to read—" And to his horror, he sobbed.

T HE BABY IS ASLEEP, AND FROM THE ELECTRONIC INTERCOM, THE mate to which is on a bracket in the doorway between Karen's and Davy's rooms in the other house, nothing comes but a soft 60-cycle hum. Their wives have not yet returned from bowling. It is peaceful there. They have drinks. Smitty sprawls half-off a couch. Herb is watching the television set, which happens to be turned off, but the easy-chair in which he is enfolded is so placed that it is a physical impossibility comfortably to look anywhere else. So on the blank screen he is looking at his thoughts. Occasionally he voices one . . . "Smitty?"

"Uh."

"Say certain words to a woman, everything goes black."

". . . talkin' about?"

" 'Differential'," says Herb.

Smitty rotates on a buttock far enough to get both feet on the floor and almost far enough to be sitting up.

" 'Transmission'," Herb murmurs. " 'Potential'."

"Transmission *what*, Herb?"

" 'Frequency' is another one. What I mean, you take a perfectly good woman, good sense and everything. Runs an Italian finesse in bridge without batting an eye. Measures formula to the drop and sterilizes it to the second. Maybe even got an automatic timer in her head, can take out a four-minute egg at exactly four minutes without a clock. What I mean, has intuition, intelligence, plenty."

"So okay."

"Okay. Now you start explaining something to her that has one of these blackout words in it. Like here at last you can buy a car with a gadget on it that locks both rear wheels in such a way that they turn together, so you can pull out of a spot where one wheel is on ice. So maybe she's read about it in an ad or something, she asks you about it. You say, well, it just cuts out the differential effect. As soon as you say the word you can see her black out. So you tell her the differential is nothing complicated, it's these gears at the back of the drive shaft that make it possible for the rear wheel at the outside of a turn to rotate faster than the wheel at the inside. But all the while you're talking you can see she is blacked out, and she will stay blacked out until you get off the subject. Frequency, too."

"Frequency?"

"Yeah, I mentioned it the other day and Jeanette like blacked out, so for once I stopped and said hey, just what is frequency anyway. Know what she said?"

"No; what she said?"

"She said it was part of a radio set."

"Well, hell, women."

"You don't get what I'm shootin' at, Smitty. Well hell women, hell! You can't dismiss it like that."

"I can. It's a lot easier."

"Well it bothers me, that's all. Word like 'frequency' now; it's good English. It says what it means. 'Frequent' means often, 'frequency' means how often something happens. 'Cycles'—that's another blackout word—means what it says too: from the top around to the top again. Or maybe from forth to back to forth again, which amounts to the same thing. But anyway, you say a frequency of eight thousand cycles per second to a woman and she blacks out twice in a row simultaneously."

"Well they just don't have technical minds."

"They don't? Did you ever hear them talking about clothes, the gores and tucks and double french seams and bias cuts? Did you ever see one of them working one of those double-needle switchback oscillating-bobbin self-fornicating sewing machines? Or in the office for that matter, running a double-entry bookkeeping machine?"

"Well, I still don't see what's so wrong if they don't bother to think through what a differential is."

"Now you got your finger on it, or near it anyway! 'They don't bother to think it through.' They don't want to think it through. They can—they can handle much more complicated things—but they don't *want* to. Now, *why*?"

"Guess they think it's unladylike or something."

"Now why the hell should that be unladylike? They got the vote, they drive cars, they do a zillion things men used to do."

"Yours not to reason why," Smitty grunts, and unfolding from the couch, he picks up his empty glass and comes for Herb's. "All I know is, if that's the way they want it, let'm. You know what Tillie got yesterday? Pair desert boots. Yeah, exactly like mine. What I say is, let'm have their goddam blackout words. Maybe then by the time my kid grows up, that'll be the way he can tell which one is his father, so *vive la différence*."

*T*hey brought him from the operating room to a place which they assured him was his own, and bade him good-bye in a way so ancient it preceded the phrase itself; it was the "God be with you" from which good-bye evolved. It was Charlie's first encounter with their word for God and their way of using it, and he was impressed.

He lay alone in a rather small room, tastefully decorated in shades of blue. One entire wall was window, overlooking the park-like landscape and the uneasily-tottering Science One. The floor was a little uneven, like many of those he had seen here, slightly resilient and obviously waterproof, so designed that it obviously could be cleaned by flooding. At the corner, and in three places about the room, the floor reached upward in mushroom, or soft boulder contours to form seating arrangements, and the corner one could be altered by pressure on a small panel to be wider, narrower, higher, or possessed of any number of bumps, grooves and protuberances, in case one should want a prop under the shoulders or knees. Three vertical golden bars by this "bed" controlled the lights; a hand placed between the first two, and raised or lowered, controlled the intensity, and a hand similarly slid between the second two ran the whole spectrum of color. An identical arrangement was placed near the door—or more properly, the unbroken wall which had in it a segment which dilated open when one gestured at a distinctive squiggle in the swirling design imprinted on the surface. The bed wall leaned inward, the opposite one out, and there were no square corners anywhere.

He appreciated their understanding thoughtfulness in giving him this needed privacy in which to pull himself together; he was grateful, angry, comfortable, lonesome, scared, curious and indignant, and such a stew must cool before anything could precipitate.

It was easy at first to whistle a whimsy in this dark: he had lost a world, and good riddance; what with one thing and another, he'd been getting pretty sick of it, and if he had ever thought there was a way of getting out of it alive, he might have wished for it.

He wondered what was left of it. Did we get the war? What lives in the Taj Mahal now—termites or alpha particles? Did that clown win the election after all, God forbid?

"Mom, did you die?"

Charlie's father had been so proud when he was born, and he had planted a redwood tree from seed. A redwood tree in Westfield, New Jersey! in the midst of a chicken-run, job-lot, shingle-and-lath type of development project, fiendishly designed to be obsolescent ten years before the mortgage could be paid off; he had visualized it towering three hundred feet high over the ruins. But then he had inexcusably dropped dead, with his affairs in such a mess and his life-insurance premiums unpaid, that Charlie's mother had sold the few spoonsful of equity he had built up in it, and had moved away. And when Charlie was seventeen, he had gone back, moved by he knew not what, on a sort of pilgrimage; and though he had never known his father, finding the house still there, finding it a slum as his father had predicted, and finding the tree alive and growing, he had done a strange thing; he had touched the tree and he had said, "It's all right, Dad." Because Mom had never known need or a day of worriment while he lived, and had he lived, she might never have known them; but in some way she seemed convinced that he knew, trouble by trouble, scrape by scrape, humiliation by hardship, what she was going through, and inside, she seemed to feel as a woman might whose man was steadily beating the love out of her and all the tolerance. So in some vague way Charlie felt he had to go and say that to the tree, as if his father lived in it like a god damned hamadryad or something;

he found it very embarrassing to remember the thing at all, but he remembered, he remembered.

Because that tree could be big now. Or if enough time had gone by, it could be dead. . . . If the Texas redhead was a wart-nosed old madam in some oil seaport by now, the tree would be pretty darn big, and if Ruth (what the hell ever happened to Ruth?) was dead and gone, the tree might be the biggest thing in the whole North Jersey complex.

All right; now he knew one of the things he had to find out. *How far? How long ago?* (Not that it would make too much difference. Would it be twenty years, and the world changed and hostile but still too much the same, like Rip van Winkle's? Or if it were a hundred, or a thousand, what real difference would that make to him?) Still: the first thing he had to find out was, *How far?*

And the next thing had to do with he, himself, Charlie Johns. As far as he had been able to find out so far, there was nothing like him here, only those Ledom, whatever the hell they were. And—what were they?

He remembered a thing he had read somewhere: was it Ruth Benedict? Something about no item of man's language, or religion, or social organization, being carried in his germ cell. In other words you take a baby, any color, any country, and plank it down anywhere else, and it would grow up to be like the people of the new country. And then there was that article he saw containing the same idea, but extending it throughout the entire course of human history; take an Egyptian baby of the time of Cheops, and plank it down in modern Oslo, and it would grow up to be a Norwegian, able to learn Morse code and maybe even have a prejudice against Swedes. What all this amounted to was that the most careful study by the most unbiassed observers of the entire course of human history had been unable to unearth a single example of human evolution. The fact that humanity had come up out of the caves and finally built an elaborate series of civilizations was beside the point; say it took them thirty thousand years to do it; it was a fair bet that a clutch of modern babies, reared just far enough to be able to find their own food and then cast into the wilderness, might well take just as long to build things up again.

Unless some evolutionary leap, as huge as the one that had produced homo sap. in the first place, had occurred again. Now, he knew nothing yet about the Ledom—nothing to speak of; yet it was clear a) that they were humans of some sort and b) they were drastically unlike any humans of his time. The difference was more than a social or cultural difference—much more than the difference, say, between an Australian aborigine and an agency executive. The Ledom were physically different in many ways, some subtle, some not. So say they evolved from humanity; was that a clue to Item One: *How far*? Well, how long does a mutation take?

He didn't know that, but he could look out of his window (staying a respectful three paces away from it) and see some scores of bright flecks moving about in the parkland below; they were, or seemed to be, adults, and if their generations were the thirty years or so one thought of when one thought of generations, and if they did not lay eggs like a salmon and then hatch them all, why, they seemed to have been around for quite a while. To say nothing of their technology: how long does it take to get the bugs out of a design like the Science One yonder? . . . That was a much harder question to answer. He remembered reading an ad in a magazine listing ten quite common items on a shopping list, aluminum foil, an antibiotic ointment, milk in cartons, and the like, and pointing out that not a single one of these things could be had twenty years ago. If you lived in a technology like that of the mid-twentieth century, you were there to see the vacuum tube displaced by the transistor and that by the tunnel diode, while in one ten-year period the artificial satellite moved from the area of laughable fantasy to a hunk of hardware broadcasting signals from the other side of the sun. Maybe he was as funny as the West Indian lady on the escalator, but he shouldn't overlook the fact that her first escalator, strange as it was to her, wasn't even a product of her future.

So hang on to that, he told himself urgently. Be not too amazed.

There were a lot of people living in his time who never did latch on to the idea that the curve of technological progress was not a flat slanting line like a diving board, but a geometrical curve like a skijump. These wistful and mixed-up souls were always suffering from attacks of belated conservatism, clutching suddenly at this dying thing and that, trying to keep it or bring it back. It wasn't real conservatism at all, of course, but an unthought longing for the dear old days when one could predict what would be there tomorrow, if not next week. Unable to get the big picture, they welcomed the conveniences, the miniaturization of this and the speed of that, and then were angrily confused when their support of these things changed their world. Well he, Charlie Johns, though he made no pretense of being a bigdome, seemed always to have been aware that progress is a dynamic thing, and you had to ride it leaning forward a little, like on a surfboard because if you stood there flat-footed you'd get drowned.

He looked out again at the Science One, and its unlikely stance seemed like an illustration of what he had been thinking. You'll have to lean strange ways to ride this one, he told himself . . . which brought him back to the formulation of Question Two.

He mustn't waste his time now wondering *how* it had been done—how he had been snatched from the worn wooden steps between the second and third floors of 61 North 34th St., in his 27th year. *How* was certainly a matter of their technology, and he couldn't be expected to figure that out. He could hope to learn how, but not to deduce it. What he had to know was—*why*?

That broke itself down into a couple of compartments. He had a right to be biased, and assume that getting him here was a large and important undertaking—but it was a fair assumption. Finagling with space and time could hardly be small items. So there was this to consider: why had this large and important thing been done? that is to say, what were the Ledom getting out of it? . . . Well, it could be purely a test of their equipment: you got a new fish-lure, you try it out just to see what it will catch. Or: they needed a specimen, any old specimen, from exactly or about his portion of time and space, so they dredged it and it happened to be

Charlie Johns. Or: they wanted Charlie Johns and no other, so they upped and got him. And this last, though logically the least likely, he unabashedly found easiest to believe. So Question Two resolved itself, *Why me?*

And Question Three followed as a corollary: *With me, what?* Charlie Johns had his faults, but he had, as well, a fairly balanced estimate of himself. He hadn't been snatched for his beauty nor his strength nor his intelligence, he was sure, because the Ledom could have done better in any or all departments, right there in his neighborhood. Nor was it for any special skill; Charlie used to say of himself that the only reason he wasn't a bum was that he worked all the time, and maybe he was a bum anyway. He had left high school in the tenth grade one time when Mom got sick, and what with one thing and another he never went back. He had sold ladies' underwear, refrigerators, vacuum cleaners and encyclopedias door to door; he had been a short-order cook, elevator operator, puddler in a steel mill, seaman, carnival shill, bulldozer operator, printer's devil and legman for a radio station. In between times he had swamped on tractor-trailers, sold papers, posted outdoor advertising, painted automobiles, and once, at a world trade fair, he had made a living for a while smearing soft-fried egg-yolk on dishes so a demonstration dishwashing machine could wash it off. He had, always, read everything and anything he could get his hands on, sometimes at wild random and sometimes on the recommendation, knowingly or not, of someone he had been talking to; for furiously, wherever he went, he struck up conversations and picked people's brains. His erudition was wide and also full of holes, and sometimes his speech showed it; he would use words he had read and not heard, and was always barking his tongue on them. For example he had for years pronounced the word "misled" as "mizzled." For a reason which demonstrates the clarity of his logic if nothing else: as a child he had seen on a box of English biscuits the picture of a trumpeter, from whose instrument came a staff of music with the staff drawn in wavy lines, probably to convey the idea of a fanfare *in vibrato*. Directly under and beside the staff was the legend "Don't be misled"; to Charlie, "mizzled" meant to be sort of wobbly and confused, like those lines. It was amazing how many people, for how long, caught his meaning when he used this word.

So . . . he was what he was, and for that, or for some of it, he had been reeled out of his world into this one. And that compartmented, too:

Either their purpose was to get him here, or—it was to get him away from there!

He mused on this. What had he been, or what had he been doing—or about to do—that the future didn't want him to be or do?

"Laura!" he cried aloud. It was just beginning, it was real, it was forever. Could that be it? because if it was, he was going to find a way and then he was going to wreck this world, if he had to blow it up like a balloon and stick a hole in it.

Because look: If he were in the future, brought there to prevent something he was about to do in the past, and if it involved Laura, then the thing they wanted to prevent was probably any more Laura; and the only way that could have been worth their while was if Laura and he had a child or children. Which meant (he had read enough science fiction to be able easily to follow such a conjecture) that in *some* existence, some time-stream or other, he had in fact married Laura and had children by her; and it was this they had decided to interfere with.

"Oh God, Laura!" he cried . . . she had not-quite red, not-quite blonde hair so that if you said apricot it would be too bright a name for the color; her eyes were brown, but so light in shade that it was the brown you use for gold when you haven't got gold paint. She defended herself fairly and clean, without any coyness or come-on, and when she surrendered it was with all her heart. He had wanted a lot of girls since he had discovered there was more to them than giggling, tattling and shrieks. He had loved a few. He had had more than a few—more than his share, he sometimes thought—of the ones he had wanted. But he had never (until Laura) had a girl he loved. It was like that thing with Ruth, when he was only fourteen. Something always happened. At these times— there had been a number of them—he had wanted the girl he loved more than anything else in life, except one thing, and that was: not to spoil it. . . . He had had fantasies, from time to time, about that, about a gathering of the four or five girls with whom this had happened, how they got their heads together to figure out why, loving them—and they knew he did, each one of them—why he had backed off. And how they would never, never be able to figure it out. Well, girls, that was the answer, take it or leave it, the simple answer: I didn't want to spoil it.

Until now.

"Now!" he cried aloud, startling himself. What the hell did "now" mean?

. . . until Laura, until that kind of whole-hearted surrender. Only you couldn't call that surrender, because he surrendered too; they both did, all at once, altogether. Just that once; and then on the way home, on the stairs . . .

Question Two was *why me*? "You better have a damn good reason," he muttered to the distant, tilted Science One. And it led to Question Three: *With me, what*? and its breakdown: he must go on, somehow, in this place—and he felt that that would almost certainly be it—or he would be able to go back. He had to find out about that.

He had to start finding out right now. He put his hand across all three of the bars that controlled the lights, and the door dilated.

"Feel better?" said Philos.

OFF-SCREEN AN IMP-CHORUS SHOUTS "GOOZLE GOOZLE" IN unison, and then with what sounds like ashcan lids, goes Wham Wham. On screen is a face: smooth, shiny-full-lipped, thick arch eyebrows, and arch is the word but (and "but" here is unavoidable) sideburns down to *here*, and a thick muscular neck sticking out of the collar of an open black leather jacket.

> Goozle Goozle
> > (*Wham Wham*)
> Goozle Goozle
> > (*Wham Wham*)
> Goozle Goozle
> > (Wham-   ) but instead of the *wham* for which

one is tensed (Smitty's television has a sound system on it of immense authority, and that *wham* has a subsonic that scares you) the heavy fringe of lashes round the pale eyes, comes up and the voice cuts in, an unhurried and unsexed voice, singing a tune. The words are something about Yee Ooo: I hold Yee Ooo, I kiss Yee Ooo, I love Yee Ooo, Ooo-Ooo. The camera dollies back and the singer is observed in a motion which one might explain by asserting that the singer, with infinite ambition, is attempting to grasp between his buttocks a small doorknob strapped to a metronome. An explosion of hysterical pipings causes the camera to cut to the front row of the audience, where a gaggle of girleens are speaking in tongues and shuddering from the internal impact of their own gender. Back to the singer who is (this must be the case) riding offstage upon an invisible model of that bicycle-like exercising machine the handlebars of which go forward and back while the pedals go high-stepping round and round and the saddle, the saddle goes up and down.

Smith casts a long arm, hooks the control, and twitches the TV set dead. "Jesus."

Herb Raile leans back in his big chair, closes his eyes, lifts his chin and says, "Sensational."

"*What?*"

"He's got something for everybody."

"You *like* it!" Smith's voice cracks on the second word.

"I never said that," says Herb. He opens his eyes and glares with mock ferocity at Smith. "And don't you ever quote me I said I did, hear?"

"Well you said *something*."

"I said he is sensational, which I allow you'll allow."

"I'll allow."

"And I said he's got something for everybody. The jailbait speaks for itself—"

"Squeaks."

Herb laughs. "Hey, I'm the copy expert here. . . . Squeak to me of love. Hey I can use that . . . and those who are moved by feelings of overt or latent homosexuality, find an object. And the young bulls like his actions and his passions and are willing to copy the D.A. haircut and the jacket. And the women, especially the older ones, like him best of all; it's the baby face and the flower eyes that does it." He shrugs. "Something for everybody."

"Forgot to mention your old neighbor buddy Smith," says Smith.

"Well, everybody needs something to hate, too."

"You're not really kiddin', Herb."

"Not really, no."

"You bother me, boy," says Smith. "When you get like this you bother me."

"Like what?"

"Like you get all serious."

"Is bad?"

"Man should take his work seriously. Shouldn't take himself seriously, how he feels and all."

"What happens to the man?"

"He gets dissatisfied." Smith looks at Herb owlishly. "Man's in advertising, say, gets serious about products, say, does serious product research on his own time. Subscribes to, say, *Consumer Reports*. Gets feelings and takes them seriously. Gets an account, can't take his work seriously."

"Put down the big gun, Smitty," says Herb, but he is a little pale. "Man picks up a new account, that's the most serious thing."

"Everything else, kicks."

"Everything else, kicks."

Smith waves at the TV set. "I don't like it and nobody's going to like it."

It comes to Herb Raile then who sponsored that rock and roll show. A competitor. Smith's competitor Number One. Oh God me and my huge mouth. Wish Jeanette was here. She wouldn't have missed that. He says, "I *said* it was a lousy show and I didn't like it."

"So you got to say it *first*, Herbie, so you get understood." He takes Herb's glass and goes away to build one more. Herb sits and thinks like an ad man should. One: the customer is always right. Two: But give me a single package from which comes all the odors of all the sins of all the sexes and I shall move the earth. And that—he glances at the great dead cataract of the dead TV eye— that was damn near it.

"*I* *feel bad, real bad*," said Charlie Johns. He was aware that though in speaking Ledom, he did it the way one should speak in a foreign tongue—that is, to think in that language before speaking—his English idiom came through quaintly, like a Frenchman's engaging "is it not?"s and "but yes"s.

"I understand," said Philos. He came all the way into the room and poised near one of the built-in, or grown-on mushroom hassocks. He had changed to an orange and white striped arrangement like wings which sprang from his shoulders on stays of some sort; they swung free behind him. His well-knit body was, except for matching shoes and the ubiquitous silken sporran, otherwise uncovered. "May I?"

"Oh sure, sit down, sit down. . . . You do *not* understand."

Philos raised a quizzical eyebrow. His eyebrows were thick and seemed level, but when he moved them, which was often, one could see that they were slightly peaked, each separately, like two furry almost flat ridged roofs.

"You're—*home*," said Charlie.

He thought for an uncomfortable flash of time that Philos was going to take his hand in sympathy, and he stirred. Philos did not, but carried quite as much sympathy in his voice. "You will be too. Don't worry."

Charlie raised his head and looked carefully at him. He seemed to mean what he said, and yet. . . . "You mean I can go back?"

"I can't answer that. Seace—"

"I'm not asking Seace, I'm asking you. Can I be sent back?"

"When Seace—"

"I'll handle Seace when the time comes! Now you square with me: can I be sent back, or not?"

"You can. But—"

"But hell."

"But you might not want to."

"And why not?"

"Please," said Philos, and his wings quivered with his earnestness, "Don't be angry. Please! You have questions—urgent questions—I know that. And what makes them urgent is that you have in your mind the answers you want to hear. You will be more and more angry if you do not get those answers, but some can't be given as you would hear them, because they would not be true. And others . . . should not be asked."

"Says *who*?"

"You! You! You will agree that some should not be asked, when you know us better."

"I will like hell. But let's just try some out and get this ice broken. You will answer them?"

"If I can, of course." (Here again was a grammatical shift. His "If I can" meant almost the same as "if I am able," but there was a shadow of "if I am enabled" in it. On the other hand—was he merely saying he would answer if he had the information? which after all is what "enables" an answer.) Charlie put the thought aside, and gave him the urgent Question One.

"How far did you come? . . . How do you mean?"

"Just what I said. You took me from the past. How long ago was that?"

Philos seemed genuinely at a loss. "I don't know."

"You don't know? Or—no one knows?"

"According to Seace—"

"Up to a point," said Charlie in exasperation, "you're right; some of these questions will have to wait, at least until I see that Seace."

"You're angry again."

"No I'm not. I'm still angry."

"Listen," said Philos, leaning forward. "We are a—well, a new people, we Ledom. Well, you'll learn all that. But you can't expect us to count time as you do, or continue some method of months and numbered years that has nothing to do with us. . . . And how can it really matter—now? How can you care at all how long it has been, when your world is finished, and only ours is left to go on?"

Charlie turned pale. "Did you say . . . finished?"

Sadly, Philos spread his hands. "Surely you realized . . ."

"What could I realize!" Charlie barked; then plaintively, "But-but-but . . . I thought maybe somebody . . . even very old . . ." The impact wouldn't come all at once, but flickered about him in flashes of faces—Mom, Laura, Ruth—and changing massive chords of darkness.

Philos said gently, "But I told you you could go back and be what you were born to be."

Charlie sat numbly for a time, then slowly turned to the Ledom. "Really?" he said, pleadingly, like a child promised the impossible—but promised.

"Yes, but then you'll be there knowing . . ." Philos made an inclusive gesture, "all you'll know."

"Oh hell," said Charlie, "I'll be home—that's the thing." But something inside him was looking at a new-found coal of terror, was breathing on it, making it pulsate bright and brighter. To know about the end—when it was coming, how it was coming; to know, as man has never known before, that what was coming really was *the* end, was *it*. . . .You lie down beside Laura's warm body knowing it. You buy Mom's lousy tabloid newspaper that she believes every word of, knowing it. You go to church (maybe pretty often, knowing it) and watch a wedding go by with the white-silk confection sitting so close to the button-busting groom midst a roaring sea of happy car-horns, knowing it. Now in this crazy off-balance place they wanted to tell him just when, just how.

"I tell you what," he said hoarsely, "you just send me back and just don't tell me when or how. Okay?"

"You are bargaining? Then will you do something for us?"

"I—" Charlie made a fumble at the sides of his hospital gown, but there were no pockets to turn out empty, "—I got nothing to bargain with."

"You have a promise to bargain with. Would you make a promise, and keep it, to get that?"

"If it's that kind of promise I could keep."

"Oh, it is, it is. It's just this: Know us. Be our guest. Learn Ledom from top to bottom—its history (there isn't much of that!), its customs, its religion and reason for being."

"That could take forever."

Philos shook his dark head, and in his black eyes, the lights gleamed. "Not too long. And when we feel you really know us, we will tell you, and you'll be free to go back. *If you want to*."

Charlie laughed. "That's an *if*?"

Soberly, Philos answered him: "I think it is."

Just as soberly, Charlie Johns said, "Let's look at the fine print, friend. The clause about 'not too long' bothers me. You could claim that I didn't know all about Ledom when it turns out I haven't counted every molecule in every eyeball in the place."

For the first time Charlie saw the flush of anger in a Ledom face. Philos said levelly, "We would not do anything like that. We do not and I think we could not."

Charlie felt his own anger stir. "You're asking me to take a hell of a lot on faith."

"When you know us better—"

"You want me to make promises *before* I know you better."

Surprisingly, engagingly, Philos sighed and smiled. "You are right—for you. All right then—no bargains now. But pay attention: I offer this, and Ledom will stand by it: if, during your examination of us and our culture, you find yourself satisfied that we are showing you everything, and that we are progressing with the disclosure fast enough to suit you, you may make the promise to see it through. And at the end, when we are satisfied that you have seen enough to know us as we would have you know us—then we will do whatever you wish about sending you back."

"Hard to argue with a deal like that. . . . And just for the record, suppose I never do make that promise?"

Philos shrugged. "You'll probably be returned to whence you came in any case. To us, the important thing is to have you know us."

Charlie looked long into the black eyes. They seemed guileless. He asked, "Will I be able to go anywhere, ask any question?"

Philos nodded.

"And get answers?"

"Any answer we are [enabled] to give."

"And the more questions I ask, the more places I go, the more I see, the sooner I get to leave?"

"Exactly so."

"I'll be damned," said Charlie Johns to Charlie Johns. He rose, took a turn around the room, while Philos watched him, and then sat down again. "Listen," he said, "before I called you in here I had myself a think. And I thought up three big questions to ask you. Mind you, in thinking them up, I didn't know what I know now— that is, that you were prepared to cooperate."

"Try them, then, and be sure."

"I mean to. Question One we have been over. It was, From how long in the future—my future—did I come." He held up a quick hand. "Don't answer it. Aside from what you've said, which isn't much but which seems to be that Seace is the one to answer such questions, I don't want to know."

"That's—"

"Shush a minute until I tell you why. First of all, it might be a tipoff as to when the end came, and I honestly don't ever want to know that. Second, now that I think of it, I can't see it would make any difference. If I go back—hey: are you sure I would go back to the very place and time I started from?"

"Very close to it."

"Okay. If that's so, it can't matter to me whether that's a year or ten thousand years back. And in the meantime I'd as soon not think of my friends old or my friends dead, or any of that: when I go back I'll be with my friends again."

"You'll be with your friends again."

"All right: so much for Question One. Question Three is also answered; it was, What is going to happen to me here?"

"I'm glad it's answered."

"All right; that leaves the one in the middle. Philos: *Why me?*"

"I beg your—"

"Why me? Why *me?* Why didn't you find someone else for your body-snatching? Or if it had to be me, why did you bother? Was it that you were testing your equipment and took what came? Or do I have some special quality or skill or something that you need? Or—did you, oh *damn* you! did you do it to stop me from doing something back then?"

Philos recoiled from him and his vehemence—not so much in fear, but in surprise and distaste, as one might step back from a burst sewer pipe.

"I shall try to answer all of those questions," he said coolly, having given Charlie thirty seconds of silence to hear the unpleasant echoes of his own voice, and to be sure he was finished. "First of all, it was you and only you we took, or could have taken. Second: yes, we were after you especially, for a special quality you have. The last part is, you'll surely agree with me, ridiculous, illogical and hardly worth your anger. For look: (the "look" was "Attend: reason this out: Observe: reflect.") In view of the fact that you have every chance of being returned to almost exactly whence you came, how could your removal possibly affect your subsequent acts? Very little time will have passed."

Glowering, Charlie thought that over. "Well," he said at length, "maybe you're right. But I'll be different, wouldn't you say?"

"From knowing us?" Philos laughed pleasantly. "And do you really and truly believe that knowledge of us can seriously affect you as you were?"

In spite of his wishes, an answering grin tugged at the corner of Charlie's mouth. Philos had a good laugh. "I guess it can't. All right." Much more agreeably, he asked, "Then would you mind telling me what's so special I've got that you need?"

"I do not mind at all." (It was one of the times when Charlie's idiom came out sounding quaint, and Philos was clearly, but with friendliness, imitating him.) "Objectivity."

"I'm sore and I'm bewildered and I'm lost. What the hell kind of objectivity is that?"

Philos smiled. "Oh, don't worry: you qualify. Look: did you ever have the experience of having an outsider—and not necessarily any kind of a specialist—say something about you that taught you something about yourself—something you couldn't have known without the remark?"

"I guess everyone has." He was reminded of the time he heard the voice of one of his minor-episode girl-friends coming unmistakably through the thin partition of a bathhouse at South Beach— and she was talking about him!—saying, "—and the first thing he'll say to you is that he never went to college, and he long ago got so used to competing with college graduates that he doesn't bother to find out anymore whether or not." It was not a large thing nor too painfully embarrassing, but never again did he mention the matter of college to anyone; for he hadn't known he *always* said it, and he hadn't known how silly it sounded.

"Well, then," said Philos. "As I told you, we are a new race, and we make it our business to know everything we can about ourselves. We have tools for this purpose that I couldn't even describe to you. But the one thing, as a species, we can't have, and that is objectivity."

"That may be all very well, but I'm no expert at observing races or species or cultures or whatever it is you're driving at."

"You *are*, though. Because you're different. That alone makes you an expert."

"And suppose I don't like what I observe?"

"Don't you see," said Philos urgently, "that does not matter? Liking or not liking us will be only facts among facts. We wish to know what becomes of what you see when it is processed by what you think."

"And once you have it—"

"We know ourselves better."

Wryly, Charlie said, "All you'll know is what *I* think."

Just as wryly, Philos said "We can always take exception. . . ."

At last, they laughed together. Then, "Okay," said Charlie Johns. "You're on." He delivered a mighty yawn and excused himself. "When do we start? First thing in the morning?"

"I thought we—"

"Look," Charlie pleaded, "I've had a long day, or whatever it was, and I'm beat."

"You're tired? Oh well, then, I don't mind waiting while you rest some more." Philos settled himself more comfortably in his seat.

After a moment of perplexed silence, Charlie said, "What I mean is, I have to get some sleep."

Philos sprang up. "Sleep!" He put a hand to his head, struck it. "I do apologize; I'd quite forgotten. Of course! . . . how do you do it?"

"Huh?"

"We don't sleep."

"You don't?"

"How do you do it? The birds put their heads under their wings."

"I lie down. I close my eyes. Then I just—lie there, that's all."

"Oh. All right. I'll wait. About how long?"

Charlie looked at him askance; he could be kidding. "Usually about eight hours."

"Eight *hours*!" and immediately, courteously, as if ashamed for having shown either ignorance or curiosity, Philos moved toward the door. "I'd better leave you alone to do it. Would that be all right?"

"That would be fine."

"If you should want anything to eat—"

"Thanks, they told me about that when they told me how to work the lights, remember?"

"Very well. And you'll find clothes in the closet here." He touched, or almost touched, a swirl in the wall-print opposite. A door dilated and slammed shut again. Charlie got a glimpse of shatteringly brilliant fabrics. "Pick out what you like best. Ah . . ." he hesitated . . . "you'll find them all . . . ah, concealing, but we've tried to design them as comfortably as possible in spite of that. But you see . . . none of the people have ever seen a male before."

"You're—females!"

"Oh—no!" said Philos, waved and was gone,

Sᴍɪᴛʜ ʀᴜɴꜱ ᴛᴏ Oʟᴅ Bᴜᴄᴄᴀɴᴇᴇʀ, Hᴇʀʙ Rᴀɪʟᴇ ᴏʙꜱᴇʀᴠᴇꜱ, ꜱᴛᴀɴᴅ-ing in Smith's downstairs bathroom and looking into the medicine chest. The medicine chest is on the wall over the toilet, and there is another chest over the vanity shelf, which is beside the sink. All these houses have the two chests. In the prospectus they were labelled *His* and *Hers*. Jeanette called them *His* and *Ours*, and apparently Tillie Smith is (in Herb's earlier phrase) moving in as well, for one and a half of the four shelves are cluttered with feminalia. As for the rest, there is Old Buccaneer Erector Set, which makes the beard stand up before shaving, and Old Bucca-neer Captain's Orders, which makes the hair lie down after combing. Also Old Buccaneer Tingle, a bath oil with added Vitamin C. (Herb one time got a huge yuk out of a dictionary definition of buccaneer: a sea robber, and said no wonder they have to put more of the stuff in it, but it was not the kind of joke that makes Smitty laugh.) Personally Herb is a little sorry for Smitty to be stuck with all that Old Buccaneer, because there is better stuff on the market. Sleek Cheek for example. Herb owes much of his altitude at the agency to the fact of having authored Sleek Cheek's slogan: a picture of a Latin American wolf (carefully continental, if your tastes were transatlantic) rubbing jowls with an ecstatic and mammariferous memsahib, over the legend *You wan' a sleek cheek?*

Well! Herb says, almost aloud. A tube of pile ointment.

Tranquilizers of course, buffered aspirins and a bottle of monstrous half-blue, half-yellow capsules. *One three times a day.* Achromycin, Herb is willing to bet. Carefully touching nothing, he leans forward to peer at the label. The date tells him that it was bought three months ago. Herb thinks back. That was about the time Smitty quit drinking for a while.

Prostate, hey?

Colorless lipstick—for chapped lips. Colorless nail polish. Touch stick. What the hell is a touch stick, No. 203 Brown? He leans closer. The fine print says *For temporary retouching between applications of Touch-Tone tint.* Time marches on, Smitty. Better yet delete the comma: Time marches on Smitty.

*C*harlie remembered (*remembered, remembered*) a chant he had heard in kindergarten. He had heard it from the big kids, the kids in second grade, the girls skipping rope:

> *Hutch*-ess *Putch*-ess *bring* the *Dutch*-ess
> *Mom*-my's *going* to *have* a *ba*-by
> Not a *boy*
> Not a *girl*
> But *just* a *lit*-tle *ba*-by.

Chanting silently, he fell asleep. He dreamed about Laura. . . . They had known each other such a little time, and yet forever; already they had a lovers' language, little terms and phrases with meaning for them and for no one else: *That's a man thing, Charlie.* He could say, "That's a woman thing, Laura," even about her shrill small squeak when the June bug got caught in her apricot hair, and make her laugh and laugh.

Waking, he went through a strange zone, coming to a place of sensibility in which he knew clearly and coldly that Laura was separated from him by impenetrable barriers of space and time, but in which, simultaneously, his mother sat at the foot of the bed. And as he passed through this zone, it became clearer and clearer to him that he was in Ledom, so that there would be none of that traveler's disorientation on fully awakening; yet with it, the sense of his mother's presence became stronger and stronger, so that when he opened his eyes and she was not there, it was as if he had seen her—she herself, not her image—disappear with an audible *pop*. Therefore, furious and injured, he awoke crying for his mother. . . .

When he had his feet under him and his head at last on top, he walked to (but not too near) the window and looked out. The weather had not changed, and he seemed to have slept the clock around, for the sky, though still overcast, was quite as bright as it had been during his trip from the Science One. He was ravenous; and, remembering his instructions, he went to the shelf-bed on which he had slept, and pulled outward on the bottom of the first of the three golden bars. An irregular section of the wall (nothing was ever square, flat, vertical or exactly smooth around here) disappeared up and back rather like the cover of a rolltop desk, and as if the orifice were a comic mouth thrusting out a broad tongue, a kind of board slid outward. On it rested a bowl and a platter. In the bowl was a species of gruel. On the platter was a mound of fruit, exotically colored and exquisitely arranged to make the best artistic display of its improbable series of shapes. There were one or two honest bananas and oranges, and some grape-like things, but the others were bulging and blue, mottled, iridescent vermilion and green, and at least seven varieties of red. What he wanted more than anything else in the world, this or any other, was something cold to drink, but there was nothing like that. He sighed and picked up an orchid-colored globe, sniffed it—it smelled, of all things, like buttered toast—and tentatively bit into it. He them emitted a loud grunt of astonishment, and cast about him for something with which to wipe his face and neck. For though the fruit's skin was, to his lips, at room temperature, its juice, which emerged under considerable pressure, was icy cold.

He had to use his white gown to mop up with, after which he took up a second specimen of the orchid fruit and tried again, with gratifying results. The clear, cold juice was without pulp, and tasted like apples with an overtone of cinnamon.

He then looked at the gruel. He had never been fond of cooked cereals, but the aroma from this one was appetizing, though he could not place it. An object lay beside the bowl, a tool of some sort. In outline it was spoonlike, but actually it consisted only of a handle holding a bright blue, fine wire loop, rather like a miniature tennis racquet without strings. Puzzled, he held it by the handle and thrust the loop into the porridge. To his surprise the gruel mounded up over the wire loop as if it had had a solid spoon-bowl under it. Lifting it, he saw that the food mounded up the under-side in the same way—not one bit more, and it didn't drip. Cau-tiously he mouthed it, and found it so delicious he could not be perturbed at the rubber-sheet texture of the invisible area inside the loop. He looked at it, true, and thrust an experimental finger through it (it resisted his finger only slightly) but all the while he was rejoicing, gland by salivary gland, at the savory, sweet-spicy, and downright muscular belly-filling nature of the gruel-like food. The flavor was utterly new to him, but, gobbling until the blue wire was distorting itself against the empty bottom of the bowl, he prayerfully wished to see it again some time soon.

Content, physically at least, he sighed and rose from the bed, whereupon the board with its cargo silently slid into the opening which immediately became part of the wall. "Room service," Char-lie murmured, wagging his head in approval. He crossed to the closet Philos had shown him and palmed the squiggle in the wall design. The door dilated. The compartment was illuminated, again by that dull sourceless silver glow. Casting a wary eye on the edges of the irregular oval opening—for that thing could open and close with real enthusiasm—he peered inside, hoping to see his good brown normal United States pants. They were not there.

Instead was a row of constructions—that was the only word for it—of fabrics stiff and floppy, starched, filmy, opaque, and all of these in combinations; reds, blues, greens, yellows, fabrics which seemed all colors at once, with threads picking up one and another hue from those around them; and fabrics with no color at all, which subdued anything they overlaid. These were put together in panels, tubes, folds, drapes, creases and seams, and variously scalloped, fringed, embroidered, appliquéd and hemmed. As his eye and hand became inured to this dazzle, a certain system became manifest; the mélange could be separated, and certain internal systems removed to be inspected by themselves as garments. Some were as simple as a night-shirt—functionally speaking, though anyone sleeping in one would surely dream he was being sliced by a diffraction grating. There were nether garments too, in the form of floppy pantaloons, leotards, tight briefs, G-strings and loin-cloths, as well as kilts long and short, flowing and crinolined, skirts full and hobbled. But what was this glittering two-inch wide, eight-foot ribbon, built like a series of letter U's attached by their top ends? And how were you supposed to wear a perfect sphere of resilient black material—on your head?

He put it on his head and tried to balance it there. It was easy. He tipped his head to roll it off. It stayed where it was. He pulled at it. It wasn't easy. It was impossible. It was stuck to him. It didn't pull at his hair either; it seemed to be his scalp it was stuck to.

He went to the three gold bars, prepared to lay his hand across them to call Philos, and then paused. No, he'd get dressed before he called for help. Whatever these crazy mixed-up people turned out to be, he still felt he didn't want to resume the practice of having a woman help him get dressed. He'd quit that some years ago.

He returned to the closet. He quickly learned the knack of hanging clothes in it. They were not on hangers exactly, but if you took a garment and spread it the way you wanted it to hang, and touched it to the wall inside the door at the right, it stayed the way it was. Then you could shove it across the closet where it slid as if on a wire, only there was no wire. When you pulled it out, it collapsed and was simply an empty garment again.

He found a long piece of material shaped roughly like the outline of an hourglass, with a length of narrow ribbon at one end. The material was a satisfyingly sober navy blue, the ribbon a rich red. Now, he thought, that ought to diaper up into a pretty fair pair of trunks. He pulled off the white gown—fortunately it was open in the back, or he'd never have gotten it off over the black ball that bounced and nodded over his head with every move. He placed the ribbonless end of the blue material on his abdomen, pulled the rest between his legs and up the back, and getting hold of the ends of the ribbon, brought them around the sides, meaning to tie them together in front. But before he could do that they fused into one, with no sign of a join or seam. He tugged at the ribbon; it stretched, then came slowly back until it was snug around his waist, where it stopped contracting. Marveling, he tugged the free front end of the material up until it was tight enough to suit him in back and between the legs, then let the free end fall in a sort of apron in front. He turned and twisted, looking at it admiringly. It fitted like his own skin, and although his legs were at the sides, bare up to the waist, with only a strip of red bolting there, he was otherwise, as Philos had suggested, concealed.

As for the rest of him, he'd just as soon skip it, for, as he had learned in his brief outdoor experience, this was a tropical place. On the other hand, most of these people seemed to wear something on the top half, if only an armband or something on the shoulder blades. He mused at the clutter of finery in the closet and saw a patch of the same dark blue as the garment he was wearing. He pulled it out. It seemed to be a sort of coat or cloak, which appeared heavy but was actually feather-light, and not only was it an exact match, but it had a thin piping of the same red as the waistband of his breech-clout. Putting it on turned into a puzzle, until he realized that, like the red thing Seace had worn, it did not come over the shoulders but went under the arms instead. It had the same stand-up collar in the back, and in the front it met just over his breastbone. There was no fastening there, but it needed none; it settled softly onto his pectoral muscles and clung there. The waist was fitted, though it did not meet in front; still, it was fitted and stayed that way. The skirt was not like Seace's, pulling back and down to a swallow-tail, but was squared off at about knuckle length all the way around.

And there were shoes in the bottom of the closet; on a shelf he saw the irreducible minimum in shoes: shaped pads made to adhere to the ball of the foot and the toes, underneath, and others to fit only the heel, with nothing between. There were many others, too; thonged and buckled sandals, and sandals with ties and self-fusing ribbons and no apparent fastening at all; soft pliant knee boots of many colors, turned-up, Turkish style shoes, platforms, huaraches, and many, many others, excepting anything which might confine or cramp the foot. He let color be his guide, and sure enough, found a pair of almost weightless, chamois-like boots which exactly matched the predominantly navy, touched with crimson outfit he was wearing. He hoped they were his size . . . and they were, perfectly, beautifully; and then he realized that certainly all *these* shoes would naturally be his or anyone's size.

Pleased with himself, he tugged once again aimlessly at the ridiculous black bubble bobbing on his head, and then went to the bars and palmed them. The door dilated with a snap, and Philos walked in. (What—was he standing with his nose on it for the last eight hours?) He was wearing a spreading kilt of amaryllis yellow, matching shoes, and a black bolero, which he seemed to have put on backwards. But on him it didn't look bad. His eloquent dark face lighted up as he saw Charlie: "Dressed already? Oh, fine!" and then indescribably puckered. It was a tight expression which Charlie couldn't quite fathom.

"You think it's all right?" he asked. "I wish I had a mirror."

"Of course," said Philos. "If I may . . ." He waited. Charlie sensed that in an offhand, ritualistic way, like "Gesundheit," he was responding to the request. But—with "May I?"

"Well, sure," said Charlie, and gasped. For Philos touched his hands together—and then Philos was gone! and instead someone else stood there, resplendent in deep navy with a high collar which excellently framed his rather long face, with well-fitting trunks with a nicely-draped apron in front of them, with very handsome shoes, and even with the bare shoulders which surmounted the full jacket, and the silly black ball bobbling on its head, the figure was a pretty snorky one. Except for the face, which unaccountably did not matter to him.

"All right?" The figure vanished and Philos reappeared; Charlie stood there open-mouthed. "How did you do that?"

"Oh, I forgot—you couldn't have seen that." He extended his

hand, on which he wore a ring of bright blue metal, the same glistening blue as the wire with which Charlie had eaten his breakfast. "When I touch it with my other hand, it makes a pretty good mirror." He did so, and the handsome figure with the silly ball on its head reappeared and then vanished.

"Now that is a *gadget*," said Charlie, for he had always been fond of gadgetry. "But why on earth do you carry a mirror around with you? Can you see yourself in it too?"

"Oh no." Philos, though he still wore the puckered expression, managed to build a smile into it. "It's purely a defensive device. We seldom quarrel, we Ledom, and this is one of the reasons. Can you imagine yourself getting all worked up and contorted and illogical (the word contained the concepts for "stupid" and "inexcusable") and then coming face to face with yourself, looking at yourself exactly as you look to everyone else?"

"Cool you down some," agreed Charlie.

"Which is why one asks permission before using it on anyone before doing so. Just politeness. That's something that's as old as my kind of humanity and probably yours too. A person resents being shown himself unless he specifically wants it."

"You have quite a toy-shop here," said Charlie admiringly. "Well . . . do I pass muster?"

Philos looked him up and down and up, and the puckered expression intensified. "Fine," he said in a strained voice. "Just fine. You've chosen very well. Shall we go?"

"Look," said Charlie, "you've got some trouble or other, haven't you? If there's anything the matter with the way I look, now's the time to tell me."

"Oh well, since you ask . . . do you," (Charlie could see he was choosing his words carefully) ". . . do you care very much for that—ah—hat?"

"That, for God's sake. It's so light I almost forgot about it, and then you and the mirror thing—hell no! I touched it to my head somehow or other and I can't get it off no way."

"That's no trouble." Philos stepped to the closet, dilated it, reached inside and came out with something about the size and shape of a shoehorn. "Here—just touch it with this."

Charlie did so, and the black object tumbled to the floor where it bounced soggily. Charlie kicked it into the closet and replaced the shoe-horn thing. "What is that?"

"The de-stator? It inactivates the biostatic force in the material."

"And biostatic force is what makes these clothes stick to themselves and to me?"

"Well, yes, because this is not exactly non-living material. Ask Seace: I don't understand it myself."

Charlie peered at him. "You still got trouble. You'd better come out with it, Philos."

The pucker increased, and Charlie had not thought it could. "I'd rather not. The last time anyone thought you were funny you booted him clear across Mielwis' central chamber."

"I'm sorry about that. I was a lot more lost then than I am now. . . . So—out with it."

"Do you know what that was you were wearing on your head?"

"No."

"A bustle."

Shouting with laughter, they left the room.

They went to see Mielwis.

"T AKE THEIR TIME BOWLING," SAYS SMITH.

"Out on strike."

"A funny funny copy man." But Smith is not putting Herb down; he is laughing inside.

The silence falls. They are talked out. Herb knows that Smith knows that each knows the other is looking for something to say. Herb reflects that it's a funny thing people can't just be together without burping out words, any old words; but he does not say it aloud because Smith might think he's getting serious again.

"Cuffs going out again," says Smith after a while.

"Yeah. Millions and millions of guys getting their pants altered. What you suppose the tailor does with all the cuffs? And what happens to all the cuff material the manufacturers don't use?"

"Make rugs."

"Cost the same," says Herb, meaning the new cuffless pants.

"*Oh* yeah." Smith knows what he means.

That silence again.

Herb says, "You got much wash-n-wear?"

"A few. Everybody does."

"Who washes it and wears it?"

"Nobody," says Smith, with a touch of indignation. "Any good cleaner's got a special process by now, does a good job."

"So why wash-n-wear?"

Smith shrugs. "Why not?"

"I guess so," says Herb, knowing when to get off a subject.

The silence.

"Ol' Farrel."

Herb looks up at Smith's grunt, and sees Smith looking out and across through his picture window and the picture window of the split-level house diagonally opposite. "What's he doing?"

"TV, I guess. But dig the crazy chair."

Herb rises, crosses the room. He carries an ashtray, puts it on the table, comes back. From a hundred and thirty feet away he doesn't seem to be staring. "One of those contour chairs."

"Yeah, but *red*. In that room, how can he get a red chair?"

"Just stick around, Smitty. He'll be remodeling."

"?"

"Remember two years ago, all knotty pine and ranch type stuff, and then one day in come that big green chair of his. Inside of a week, voom. Early American."

"Oh yeah."

"So inside of a week, you watch."

"Voom."

"That's what I said."

"How can he pop for two remodeling jobs in three years?"

"Maybe he got relatives."

"You know him?"

"Me? Hell no. Never been in the place. Hardly said hello."

"Thought he was hard up though."

"Whuffo?"

"Car."

"So he spends it on remodeling."

"Queer people anyway."

"What type queer?"

"Tillie saw her buy blackstrap molasses at the super."

"Oh hell," says Herb, "it's like a cult, that stuff. No wonder about the car. Prob'ly don't even care who sees it's eighteen months old."

The silence.

Smith says, "Bout time painted this place."

Herb says, "Me too."

White lights scythe the landscaping; Smith's station wagon wheels into the drive, into the carport and dies. Car doors slam like a two-syllable word. Female voices approach, two speaking simultaneously, neither missing a thing. The door opens, Tillie comes in, Jeanette comes in.

"Hi bulls, what's bulling?"

"Just man talk," says Smith.

They walked undulating corridors and twice stepped harmlessly into bottomless pits and were whisked upwards. Mielwis, in a diagonal arrangement of wide ribbon wrapped to the right around his body and down his right leg, and wrapped to the left down around his left leg, yellow and purple, was alone and looked quite imposing. He greeted Charlie with grave cheerfulness and clearly, openly, audibly approved the navy-blue outfit.

"I'll leave you," said Philos to whom Mielwis had paid no attention whatever (which, thought Charlie, might have meant only acceptance) until he said this, nodded and smiled kindly. Charlie waved a finger, and Philos was gone.

"Very tactful," said Mielwis approvingly. "We have only one like Philos."

"He's done his best for me," said Charlie, and then added in spite of himself, "I think . . ."

"Well now," said Mielwis, "Good Philos tells me you feel much better."

"Let's just say I'm beginning to know how I feel," said Charlie, "which is more than I knew when I first got here."

"Unsettling experience." Charlie watched him carefully, in some way compelled to. He had no reference whatever as to the probable age of these people, and if Mielwis seemed older, it was probably the sum of that barely acknowledged respect which others gave him, and his slightly larger size, and fuller face, and the really extraordinary—even here—spacing of his eyes. But there was nothing about any of these people which bespoke aging as he had known it.

"So you want to find out all there is to know about us."

"I certainly do."

"Why?"

"That's my ticket home." The phrase was so idiomatic that it was nearly meaningless in the language, and Charlie knew it as soon as he said it. There seemed no concept for "payment" or "pass" in the tongue; the word he had chosen for "ticket" came out meaning "label" or "index card." "I mean," he supplemented, "I am told that when I have seen all you care to show me—"

"—and all you care to ask—"

"—and give you my reactions to it, you are prepared to put me back where I came from."

"I am pleased to be able to ratify that," and Charlie got the impression that without bragging, Mielwis was informing him that for him, Mielwis, to ratify it was a large measure. "Let us begin." Somehow that seemed like a witticism.

Charlie laughed puzzledly. "I hardly know where." Some words he had read somewhere—Charles Fort? Oh! How he'd have loved this setup!—Fort had said, "To measure a circle, begin anywhere." "All right then. I want to know about . . . something personal about the Ledom."

Mielwis spread his hands. "Anything."

Suddenly shy, he couldn't ask directly. He said, "Philos said something last night—or anyway, just before I slept . . . Philos said you Ledom had never seen the body of a male. And I immediately thought he meant you were all females. But when I asked him, he said no. Now, either you're one or the other, right?"

Mielwis did not answer, but remained still, looking at him kindly from those wide eyes and keeping a poised, also kindly, half-smile on his lips. In spite of his embarrassment, which for some reason began to be acute, Charlie recognized the technique and admired it; he'd had a teacher once who did that. It was a way of saying "Figure it out for yourself," but it would never be used on anyone who had not all the facts. Sort of like the "Challenge to the Reader" in an Ellery Queen whodunit.

Charlie jumbled together in his mind all the uneasy impressions he had had on the matter: the large (but not unusually large) pectoral development, and the size of the areolae; the absence of wide-shouldered, narrow-hipped individuals. As to other cosmetic characteristics, like the hair, worn in as many different ways as clothes, though predominantly short, and the clothes themselves with their wild variegation, he refused to be led astray.

Then he turned to the language, which so unaccountably (to him) he could speak with fluency, and yet which was constantly presenting him with mysteries and enigmas. He looked at the grave and patient Mielwis, and said to himself in Ledom: "I am looking at him." And he examined the pronoun "him" by itself for the very first time, and found that it had gender only in his own reference; when he spoke the word it translated to "him" in English because, for some reason of his own, Charlie preferred it that way. But in its own reference, in the Ledom tongue, it had no sexual nor gender meaning. Yet it was a *personal* pronoun; it would not be used in speaking of things. In English, "it" is an impersonal pronoun; the word "one" used as a pronoun is not, stilted though it may be: "One would think one was in Paradise." The personal pronoun—and there was only one! in Ledom was like that: personal and without gender. That Charlie had told himself it was "he" was Charlie's own mistake, and now he knew it.

Did the pronoun's having no gender mean the Ledom then had no sex? For that would be one way to make Philos' extraordinary remark consistent: they had never seen a male, but they were not females.

The words and concepts "male" and "female" existed in the language . . . the alternative was: *both*. The Ledom, each of them, had both sexes.

He looked up into Mielwis' patient eyes. "You're both," he said.

Mielwis did not move or speak for what seemed a very long time. Then his half-smile broadened, as if he were pleased at what he saw in Charlie's upturned face. Gently, then, he said, "Is that such a terrible thing?"

"I haven't thought whether or not it's terrible," said Charlie candidly. "I'm just trying to figure how it's possible."

"I'll show you," said Mielwis, and in his stately way he rose and came around his desk toward the stricken Charlie.

"**H**i, bulls," says Tillie Smith. "What's bulling?"

"Just man talk," says Smith.

Herb says, "Hi, bowls. What's bowling?"

Jeanette says, "Three strikes and I'm out."

"Herb already used the gag," Smith says in his leaden way, which isn't true.

Tillie tops them all: "What's everybody saying highballs for? Let's all have a drink."

"Not us," says Herb quickly, clinking ice in an otherwise empty glass. "I've had mine and it's late."

"Me too," says Jeanette because she gets the message.

"Thanks for the drinks and all the dirty jokes," Herb says to Smith.

"Let's not tell 'em about the dancing girls," says Smith.

Jeanette makes wide bowling gestures. "'Night, Til. Keep 'em rolling."

Tillie also makes bowling gestures, causing Smith to reseat himself on his shoulderblades, where he much prefers to be in any case. The Railes gather up her bowling bag, Herb grunting dramatically as he hefts it, and the baby-sitter, which Jeanette unplugs and tucks under Herb's left arm while she inserts her handbag under his right, and because she is a lady, waits for him to open the door for her with his knee.

*"C*ome this way," *Mielwis said, and Charlie rose and followed* him into a smaller room. One whole end, floor to ceiling, was a pattern of slits with labels—some sort of filing system, he presumed; and Lord preserve us, even these were not in straight lines, but in arcs . . . and come to think of it, they did resemble the arcs he had seen drawn on an assembly bench, once, by an efficiency expert: maximum reach of right hand, optimum reach of left hand, and so on. Attached to one wall was a flat white soft shelf—an examination table if ever he saw one. Mielwis, in passing, batted it gently and it followed him down the room, slowly sinking, until when it was within ten feet of the wall it was at chair height. "Sit down," Mielwis said over his shoulder.

Numbly, Charlie sat, and watched the big Ledom stand and glance over the labels. Suddenly, surely, he reached up. "Here we are." He hooked his slender fingertips in one of the slots and moved his hand downward. A chart began feeding out of the slot; it was about three feet wide and was very nearly seven feet long. As it came down the lights in the room slowly dimmed, while the picture on the chart brightened. Mielwis reached up and started a second chart and then sat beside Charlie.

The room was now totally dark, and the charts blazed with light. In full color, they were the front and side views of a Ledom, clad only in the silky sporran which began perhaps an inch under the navel and fell, widening from perhaps a palm's breadth at the top, to its lower edge, which was roughly three inches above mid-thigh, and which extended from the front of one leg to the front of the other. Charlie had seen them, already, longer and shorter than this, and also red, green, blue, purple and snowy white, but he had yet to see the Ledom who went without one. It was obviously a tight taboo, and he did not comment

"We shall dissect," said Mielwis, and by means unperceived by Charlie Johns, he caused the chart to change: *blip!* And the sporran, as well as the superficial skin under it, were gone, exposing the fascia and some of the muscle fibres of the abdominal wall. With a long black pointer he magically produced, he indicated the organs and functions he described. The tip of the pointer was a needle, a circle, an arrow and a sort of half-parenthesis at his will, and his language was concise and intimately geared to Charlie's questions.

And Charlie asked questions! His unease had long since disappeared, and two of his most deep-dyed characteristics took over: one, the result of his omnivorous, undisciplined, indefatigable reading and picking of brains; second, the great gaping holes this had left in his considerable body of knowledge. Both appeared far more drastic than he had heretofore known; he knew ever so much more than he knew he knew, and he had between five and seven times as much misinformation and ignorance than he had ever dreamed.

The anatomical details were fascinating, as such things so often are, and for the usual reason which overwhelms anyone with the vestiges of a sense of wonder: the ingenuity, the invention, the efficient complexity of a living thing.

First of all, the Ledom clearly possessed both sexes, in an active form. First of all, the intromittent organ was rooted far back in what might be called, in homo sap., the vaginal fossa. The base of the organ had, on each side of it, an os uteri, opening to the two cervixes, for the Ledom had two uteri and always gave birth to fraternal twins. On erection the phallos descended and emerged; when flaccid it was completely enclosed, and it, in turn, contained the urethra. Coupling was mutual—indeed, it would be virtually impossible any other way. The testicles were neither internal nor external, but superficial, lying in the groin just under the skin. And throughout, there was the most marvellous reorganization of the nervous plexi, at least two new sets of sphincter muscles, and an elaborate redistribution of such functions as those of Bartholin's and Cowper's glands.

When he was quite, quite satisfied that he had the answers, and when he could think of no more, and when Mielwis had exhausted his own promptings, Mielwis flicked the two charts with the back of his hand and they slid up and disappeared into their slots, while the lights came up.

Charlie sat quietly for a moment. He had a vision of Laura—of all women . . . of all men. *Biology,* he remembered irrelevantly; *they used to use the astronomical symbols for Mars and Venus for male and female. . . . What in hell would they use for these? Mars plus y? Venus plus x? Saturn turned upside down?* Then he heeled his eyes and looked up at Mielwis, blinking. "How in the name of all that's holy did humanity get *that* churned up?"

Mielwis laughed indulgently, and turned back to the rack. He (and even after such a demonstration, Charlie found himself thinking of Mielwis as "he"—which was still the convenient translation of the genderless Ledom pronoun) he began hunting up and back and down. Charlie waited patiently for new revelation, but Mielwis gave an annoyed grunt and walked to the corner, where he placed his hand on one of the ubiquitous, irregular swirls of design. A tiny voice said politely, "Yes, Mielwis."

Mielwis said, "Tagin, where have you gone and filed the homo sap. dissections?"

Came the tiny voice, "In the archives, under Extinct Primates."

Mielwis thanked the voice and went round to a second bank of slots at the side. He found what he was looking for. Charlie rose when he beckoned, and came to him, and the bench followed obediently. Mielwis tapped down more charts, and seated himself.

The lights dimmed and went out; the charts flamed. "Here are dissections of homo sap., male and female," Mielwis began. "And you described Ledom as churned up. I want to show you just how little real change there has been."

He began with a beautiful demonstration of the embryology of the human reproductive organs, showing how similar were the prenatal evidences of the sexual organs, to the end of showing how really similar they remained. Every organ in the maie has its counterpart in the female. "And if you did not come from a culture which so exhaustively concentrated on differences which were in themselves not drastic, you would be able to see how small the differences actually were." (It was the first time he had heard any of the Ledom make a knowledgeable reference to homo sap.) He went on with some charts of a pathological nature. He demonstrated how, with biochemicals alone, one organ could be made to atrophy and another actually perform a function when it itself had been vestigial to begin with. A man could be made to lactate, a woman to grow a beard. He demonstrated that progesterone was normally secreted by males, and testosterone by females, if only in limited amounts. He went on to show pictures of other species, to give Charlie an idea of how wide a variety there is, in nature, in the reproductive act: the queen bee, copulating high in midair, and thereafter bearing within her a substance capable of fertilizing literally hundreds of thousands of eggs for literally generation after generation; dragonflies, in their winged love-dance with each slender body bent in a U, forming an almost perfect circle whirling and skimming over the marshes; and certain frogs the female of which lays her eggs in large pores in the male's back; seahorses whose males give birth to the living young; octopods who, when in the presence of the beloved, wave a tentacle the end of which breaks off and swims by itself over to the female who, if willing, enfolds it and if not, eats it. By the time he was finished, Charlie was quite willing to concede that, in terms of all nature, the variation between Ledom and homo sap. was neither intrinsically unusual nor especially drastic.

"But what happened?" he asked, when he had had a chance to mull all this. "How did this come about?"

Mielwis answered with a question: "What first crawled out of the muck and breathed air instead of water? What first came down out of the trees and picked up a stick to use as a tool? What manner of beast first scratched a hole in the ground and purposely dropped in a seed? It happened, that's all. These things happen. . . ."

"You know more about it than that," accused Charlie. "And you know a lot about homo sap. too."

With a very slight touch of testiness, Mielwis said, "That's Philos' specialty, not mine. As far as the Ledom is concerned. As for homo sap., it was my understanding that you purposely wish not to know the time or nature of its demise. No one's trying to deny you information you really want, Charlie Johns, but does it not occur to you that the beginnings of Ledom and the end of homo sap. may have something to do with one another? Of course . . . it's up to you."

Charlie dropped his eyes. "Th-thanks, Mielwis."

"Talk it over with Philos. He can explain if anyone can. And I'll allow," he added, smiling broadly, "that he knows where to stop better than I do. It isn't in my nature to withhold information. You go talk it over with him."

"Thanks," Charlie said again. "I—I will."

Mielwis' parting word was to the effect that Nature, profligate though she may be, generator of transcendant and complicated blunders, holds one single principle above all others, and that is continuity. "And she will bring that about," he said, "even when she must pass a miracle to do it."

"**O**H, YOU KNOW IT'S GREAT," JEANETTE SAYS TO HERB AS she makes a couple of nightcaps (anyway) and he is returning to the kitchen after looking at the children, "it's great having neighbors like the Smiths."

"Great," says Herb.

"Like I mean interests in common."

"Do any good tonight?"

"Oh yes," she says, handing him the glass and perching against the sink. "You've been working for seven weeks on a presentation for the Big Bug Bakeries to sell a promotion on luxury ice-cream and cake shoppes." She pronounces it "shoppies."

"I have?"

"Name of store chain, *Just Desserts*."

"Oh hey, purty purty. You're a genius."

"I'm a scrounge," she says, "Tillie came out with it as a crack and maybe she'll forget she said it which is why you've been working on it for seven weeks."

"Clever clever. Will do. Smitty put me down once tonight."

"You punch him in the nose?"

"Sure. Middle-large wheel in big account. Fat chance."

"Whoppen?"

He tells her about the TV show, how he said some things that sounded like compliments for it, and it sponsored by the competition.

"Oh," she says. "You fool you, but all the same he's a wick." A wick is their personal idiom for anyone who does wicked things.

"I got out from under pretty good."

"All the same, you want to get a bomb ready just in case."

He glances out the window and across the lot. "Awful close for a bomb to go bang."

"Only if they know who dropped it."

"Aw," he says, "we don't want to bomb him."

"Course not. We just want a bomb in case. Besides, I got a bombsite it would be a shame to waste." She tells him about old Trizer who got kicked upstairs and would be so happy to roll something down on Smitty.

"Get off him, Jeannette. He got prostate."

" 'And there he lay, prostate on the floor.' He tell you?"

"No, I found out, that's all." He adds, "Piles too."

"Oh goody. I'll twig Tillie."

"You are the most vindictive female I ever heard of."

"They put my little buddy-buddy-hubby down, and I won't let'm."

"Besides, she'll think I told you."

"She'll only wonder and wonder how it ever got out. I'll fix it, buddy-buddy-hubby. We're a team, that's what."

He swirls his drink and watches it spin. "Smitty said something about that." He tells her about the desert boots and how Smitty thinks pretty soon the kids won't know which one is the father.

"Bother you?" she says brightly.

"Some."

"You forget it," she tells him. "You're hanging on to somebody's dead hand from way back. What we are, we're a new kind of people, buddy-buddy. So suppose Karen and Davy grow up without this big fat Thing you read about, the father image, the mother image, all like that."

" 'The Story of my Life, by Karen Raile. When I was a lit-tul girrul I did-unt have a mom-my and dad-dy like the other lit-tul boys and girruls, I had a Committee.' "

"Committee or no, gloomy-Gus, they have food drink clothes house and love, and isn't that supposed to be all of it?"

"Well yes, but that father image is supposed to be worth something too."

She pats him on the cheek. "Only if you way down deep feel you have to be big. And you're already sure you're the only one big enough to belong to this Committee, right? Let's go to bed."

"How do you mean that?"

"Let's go to bed."

Charlie Johns found Philos standing outside Mielwis' office,
looking as if he had just arrived. "How was it?"

"Huge," said Charlie. "It's, well, overwhelming, isn't it?" He looked
carefully at Philos, and then said, "I guess it isn't, not to you."

"You want more? Or was that enough for now? Do you have to
sleep again?"

"Oh no, not until night." The word "night" was there to be used,
but like "male" and "female," seemed to have a rather more remote
application than he needed to express himself. He thought he
ought to add to it. When it's dark."

"When what is dark?"

"You know. The sun goes down. Stars, moon, all that."

"It doesn't get dark."

"It doesn't . . . what are you talking about? The earth still turns,
doesn't it?"

"Oh, I see what you mean. Oh yes, I imagine it still gets dark
out there, but not in Ledom."

"What is Ledom—underground?"

Philos cocked his head on one side. "That isn't a yes or no kind
of question."

Charlie looks down the corridor and out one of the huge panes to
the overcast bright silver sky. "Why isn't it?"

"You'd better ask Seace about it. He can explain better than I
can."

In spite of himself, Charlie laughed, and in answer to Philos' querying look, he explained, "When I'm with you, Mielwis can supply the answers. When I'm with Mielwis, he tells me that you're the expert. And now you send me to Seace."

"What did he say I was an expert at?"

"He didn't say, exactly. He implied that you knew all there was to know about the history of Ledom. He said something else . . . let's see. Something about you knowing when to stop giving information. Yes, that was it; he said you'd know where to stop, because it isn't in his nature to withhold information."

For the second time Charlie saw a swift flush pass through Philos' dark enigmatic face. "But it's my nature."

"Oh, now, look," said Charlie anxiously, "I could be misquoting. I could have missed something. Don't make me a source of trouble between you and—"

"Please," said Philos evenly, "I know what he meant by it, and you haven't done any harm. This is one thing in Ledom which has nothing to do with you."

"It has, it has! Mielwis said that the beginning of Ledom may well have something to do with the end of homo sap., and that's the one thing I want to steer clear of. It certainly does involve me!"

They had begun to walk, but now Philos stopped and put his hands on Charlie's shoulders. He said, "Charlie Johns, I do beg your pardon. We're both—we're all wrong, and all right. But truly, there is nothing in this interchange that you're responsible for. Please let it go at that, for it was wrong of me to behave that way. Let my feelings, my problems, be forgotten."

Slyly, Charlie said, "What—and not know everything about Ledom?" And then he laughed and told Philos it was all right, and he would forget it.

He wouldn't.

IN BED, HERB SUDDENLY SAYS, "BUT MARGARET DON'T LOVE US."

Contently, Jeanette says, "So we'll bomb her too. Go to sleep. Margaret who?"

"Mead. Margaret Mead the anthropologist who had that article I told you about."

"Why she don't love us?"

"She says a boy grows up wanting to be like his father. So when his father is a good provider and playmate and is as handy around the house as a washer-dryer combination or a garbage disposer or even a wife, why the kid grows up full of vitamins and fellow-feeling and becomes a good provider and playmate and etcetera."

"So what's wrong with that?"

"She says from Begonia Drive can't come adventurers, explorers and artists."

After a silence, Jeanette says, "You tell Margaret to go climb Annapurna and paint herself a picture. I told you before—we're a new kind of people now. We're inventing a new kind of people that isn't all bollixed up with Daddy out drunk and Mommy with the iceman. We're going to bring out a whole fat crop of people who like what they have and don't spend their lives getting even with somebody. You better quit thinking serious things, buddy-buddy-hubby. It's bad for you."

"You know," he says in amazement, "that's precisely exactly what Smitty told me." He laughs. "You tell it to me to set me up, he tells it to me to put me down."

"I guess it's how you look at it."

He lies there for a time thinking about his-and-her desert boots and my parent is a Committee and how dandy a guy can be with a dish cloth, until it starts to spin a bit in his head. Then he thinks the hell with it and says, "Good night, honey."

"Good night, honey," she murmurs.

"Good night, sweetie."

"G'night, sweetie."

"God damn it!" he roars, "Stop calling me all the time the same thing I call you!"

She is not scared exactly, but she is startled, and she knows he is working something out, so she says nothing.

After a time Herb touches her and says, "I'm sorry, honey."

She says, "That's all right—George."

He has to laugh.

*I*t took only a few minutes by "subway"—there was a Ledom name for it but it was a new one and has no direct English translation—for Philos and Charlie to get to the Science One. Emerging under that toppling-top of a structure, they made their way around the pool, where thirty or forty Ledom were splashing again (it could hardly be "still") and they stood a moment to watch. There had been little talk on the way, both having apparently a sufficiency of things to think about, and it was through his own thoughts that Charlie murmured, watching the diving, wrestling, running: "What in time keeps those little aprons on?" And Philos, reaching gently, tugged at Charlie's hair and asked, "What keeps that on?"

And Charlie, for one of the very few times in his whole life, blushed.

Around the building and under the colossal overhang they went, and there Philos stopped. "I'll be here when you're through," he said.

"I wish you'd come up with me," said Charlie. "This time I'd like you to be around when somebody says, 'Talk to Philos about it.' "

"Oh, he'll say it all right. And I'll talk you blue in the face when the time comes. But don't you think you should know more about Ledom as it is before I confuse you with a lot of things about what it was?"

"What *are* you, Philos?"

"A historian." He waved Charlie over to the base of the wall and placed his hand on the invisible railing. "Ready?"

"Ready."

Philos stepped back and Charlie went hurtling upward. By this time he was familiar enough with the sensation to be able to take it without turning off the universe; he was able to watch Philos walking back toward the pool. Strange creature, he thought. Nobody seems to like him.

He drifted to a silent stop in apparent midair before the great window, and boldly stepped toward it. And through it. And again he sensed that certainty of enclosure as he did so: what did it do, that invisible wall—withdraw its edges exactly around him, so that he formed part of the enclosure while passing through? It must be something like that.

He looked around. The first thing he saw was the padded cell, the silver winged pumpkin, the time machine, with its door open just as it had been when he emerged. There were the draped ends of the room, and some kind of oddly leaning equipment on a sort of heavy stand near the center of the room; some chairs, a sort of stand-up desk with a clutter of papers on it.

"Seace?"

No answer. He walked across the room a little timidly, and sat on one of the chairs, or hummocks. He called again, a little louder, with still no results. He crossed his legs and waited, and uncrossed them and recrossed them on the other side. After a time he rose again and went to peer into the silver pumpkin.

He hadn't known it would hit him so hard; he hadn't known it would hit him at all. But there, just there on that smooth soft curved silver floor, he had sprawled, more dead than anything, years and unknown miles away from everything that ever mattered, even with the precious sweat dried on his body. His eyes burned in a spurt of tears. Laura! Laura! Are you dead? Does being dead make you any nearer where I am? Did you grow old, Laura, did your sweet body wrinkle and shrivel up? When it did, were you suddenly glad there to see it? Laura, do you know I'd give anything in life and even life itself to touch you once—even to touch you if you were old and I was not?

Or . . . did the end, the final, awful *thing* happen while you were young? Did the big hammer hit your house, and were you gone in a bright instant? Or was it the impalpable rain of poison, making you bleed inside and vomit and lift up your head and look at the lovely hair fallen out on the pillow?

How do you like me? he cried in a silent shout and a sudden soundless crash of gaiety; how do you like Charlie in navy-blue, red-piped diapers and a convertible coat with the top down? How about this crazy collar?

He knelt in the doorway of the time machine and covered his face with his hands.

After a while he got up and went looking for something to wipe his nose on.

Looking and looking, he said, "I'm going to be with you when it happens, Laura. Or until it happens. . . . Laura, maybe we can both die of old age, waiting. . . ." Blinded by his own feelings, he found himself fumbling with the drapes at one end of the room without really knowing how he got there or what he was doing. Back there was nothing but wall, but there was a squiggle, and he palmed it. An opening like the one which had contained his break-fast appeared, only no long tongue came shoving out. He bent and peered, into the illuminated interior, and saw a pile of roughly cubical transparent boxes stacked inside, and a book.

He took out the boxes, at first just curiously, then with increasing excitement. He took them out one by one, but carefully, one by one, he put them back as he had found them.

In a box was a nail, a rusty nail, with bright metal showing where it had been diagonally sheared.

In a box was a rain-faded piece of a book of matches, with the red from the match-heads staining the paper sticks. And he knew it, he knew it! He'd recognize it anywhere. It was only a fragment, but that was from Dooley's Bar and Grill over on Arch Street. Except that . . . that the few letters that were left were reversed . . .

In a box was a dried marigold. Not *flamboyante*, not one of

Ledom's crossbred bastardized beautiful miracle blossoms, but a perky little button of a driedup marigold.

In a box was a clod of earth. Whose earth? Was this earth that her foot had trodden? Did it come from the poor sooty patch of ground under the big white lantern with the fading 61 painted on it? Had the very tip of the time machine's front tooth bitten this up on an early try?

Finally, there was a book. Like everything else here, it refused to be a neat rectangle, being a casual circular affair about as precise in contour as an oatmeal cookie, and the lines inside were not-quite-regular arcs. (On the other hand, if you learned to write without shifting your elbow, wouldn't arced lines be better to write on?) But anyway it opened hingewise as a good book should, and he could read it. It was Ledom, but he could read it, which astonished him no more than his sudden ability to speak it; less, rather; he had already been astonished and that was that.

It consisted first of all of some highly technical description of process, and then several pages of columnar entries, with many erasures and corrections, as if someone had made here a record of some tests and calibrations. Then there were a great many pages each of which had received an imprint of four dials, like four clocks or instruments, minus their hands. Towards the end these were blank, but the first were scribbled and scrawled over, with the dial-hands marked in and odd notes: *Beetle sent, no return.* There were a lot of these *no return* entries, until he came to a page over which was scrawled a huge and triumphant Ledom-style exclamation point. It was Experiment 18, and shakily written was *Nut sent, Flower returned!* Charlie got out the box with the flower in it and, turning it over several times, finally located the number 18.

Those dials those dials. . . . he turned suddenly and hurried to the leaning array of unfamiliar equipment near the center of the room. Sure enough, there were four dials on it, and around the rim of each, a knob, tracked to circle the dial. Let's see, you'd set the four knobs according to the book, and then—oh sure, there it was.

A toggle switch is a toggle switch in any language, and he could read ON and OFF in this one.

Back he went to the corner, turned the pages frantically. Experiment 68 ... the last one before the unfilled pages began. *Sent Stones. Return:* (In Ledom phonetics) *Charlie Johns.*

He clutched the book hard and began to read those settings off that paper and into his head.

"Charlie? You here, Charlie Johns?"

Seace!

When Seace, having entered from some invisible dilating doorway behind the time machine, came round the corner, Charlie had been able to return the book. But he wasn't able to find the squiggle in time, and there he stood, with the compartment open and the boxed dead marigold in his hand.

"WHAT YOU DOING?"

Herb opens his eyes and sees his wife standing over him. He says, "Lying in a hammock of a Saturday noon a-talkin' to my broad."

"I was watching you. You were looking very unhappy."

"As Adam said when his wife fell out of the tree—Eve's dropping again."

"Oh, you golden bantam you! . . . tell mama."

"You and Smitty don't want me to talk serious."

"Silly. I was asleep when I said that."

"All right. I was thinking about a book I read one time which I wish I had to read over. *The Disappearance*."

"Maybe it just disappeared, then. Oh God, it's Philip Wylie. Likes fish, hates women."

"I know what you mean and you're wrong. He likes fish but hates the way women are treated."

"That makes you look unhappy in a hammock?"

"I wasn't really unhappy. I was just trying awful hard to remember exactly what the man said."

"In *The Disappearance*? I remember. It's about how all the women in the world disappeared one day, right off the earth. Spooky."

"You did read it! Oh good. Now, there was a chapter in it that kind of set out the theme. That's what I want."

"Oh-h-h-h . . . yes. I remember that. I started to read it and then I skipped it because I wanted to get on with the story. There was this—"

"The only thing I like about a copywriter that's better than a best-seller writer," Herb interrupts, "is that though they're both wordsmiths, a copywriter makes it his business to never let his words get between the customer and the product. That's what Wylie did with that chapter in that book. Nobody who needs it ever gets to read it."

"You mean *I* need it?" she says defensively, then, "What is it he's got I need?"

"Nothing," says Herb miserably, and sinks back in the hammock with his eyes closed.

"Oh, honey, I didn't mean—"

"Oh, I'm not mad. It's just, I think he agrees with you. I think he knows why he does better than you do."

"Agrees with *what*, for Pete's sake!"

Herb opens his eyes and looks past her at the sky. "He says people made their first big mistake when first they started to forget the similarity between men and women and began to concentrate on the difference. He calls that *the* original sin. He says it has made men hate men and women too. He blames it for all wars and all persecutions. He says that because of it we've lost all but a trickle of the ability to love."

She snorts. "I never said any of that!"

"That's what I was thinking so hard about. You said we were a new kind of people coming up, like a Committee or a team. The way there are girl things to do, and boy things to do, and nowadays it doesn't much matter who does 'm; we both can, or either."

"Oh," she says. "That."

"Wylie, he even makes a funny. He says some people think that most men are stronger than most women because men have bred women selectively."

"Do you breed women selectively?"

He laughs at last, which is what she wants; she can't bear to have him looking sad. "Every damn time," he says, and topples her into the hammock.

*S*eace, his head cocked to one side, came briskly down to Charlie. "Well, my young booter-in-the-tail. What are you up to?"

"I'm sorry about that," Charlie stammered. "I was very mixed up,"

"You dug out the flower, hm?"

"Well, I came and—you were, I mean weren't—"

Surprisingly, Seace clapped him on the shoulder. "Good, good; it's one of the things I was going to show you. You know what that flower is?"

"Yes," said Charlie, almost unable to speak. "It's a m-marigold."

Seace fumbled past him and got out the book, and wrote down the name of the flower. "Doesn't exist in Ledom," he said proudly. He nodded toward the time machine. "Never can tell what that thing will dredge up. Of course, you're the prize specimen. Chances are once in a hundred and forty three quadrillion of doing it again, if that makes any sense to you."

"You . . . you mean that's all the chance I have of going back?"

Seace laughed. "Don't look so woebegone! Milligram by milligram—I do believe, atom by atom—what you put in there, you take out. Question of mass. Have complete choice of what we shove in. What comes out—" He shrugged.

"Does it take long?"

"That's something I hoped to learn from you, but you couldn't say. How long do you think you were in there?"

"Seemed like years."

"Wasn't years; you'd have starved to death. But this end, it's instantaneous. Shut the door, throw the switch, open the door, it's all over." Calmly, he took the marigold from Charlie, and the book, slung them back in the hole, and palmed it shut. "Now then! What d'you want to know? I'm told I'm to draw the line only at information about when and how homo sap. cuts its silly collective throat. Sorry. Don't take that personally. Where do you want to begin?"

"There's so much . . ."

"You know something? There's precious little. Let me give you an example. Can you imagine a building, a city, a whole culture maybe, running on the single technological idea of the electric generator and the motor—which is essentially the same thing?"

"I—well, sure."

"And pretty amazing to someone who'd never known such a thing before. With just electricity and motors, you can pull, push, heat, cool, open, close, light—well, more or less, name it, you have it. Right?"

Charlie nodded.

"Right. All motion things, see what I mean? Even heat is motion when you get right down to it. Well, we have a single thing that does all that the electric motor can do, plus a whole range of things in the static area. It was developed here in Ledom, and it's the keystone to the whole structure. Called A-field. A is for Analog. A very simple-minded gadget, basically. 'Course, the theory—" He wagged his head. "You ever hear of a transistor?"

Charlie nodded. This was a man with whom one could converse with one's neck-muscles.

Seace said, "Now there's as simple-minded a device as a device can get. A little lump of stuff with three leads into it. Shove a signal in one wire, out comes the same signal multiplied by a hundred. No warm-up time, no filaments to break, no vacuum to lose, and almost no power to operate.

"Then along comes the tunnel diode and makes the transistor

complicated, overweight, oversized and inefficient in comparison, and it's much smaller and, to the naked eye, a lot simpler. But the theory, God! I've always said that some day we'll reduce these things so far that we'll be able to do anything at all with nothing at all drawing no power—only nobody'll be able to understand the theory."

Charlie, who had encountered the professorial joke before, smiled politely.

"All right: the A-field. I'll try to make it nontechnical. Remember that spoon you used this morning? Yes? Yes. Well, in the handle is a sub-miniature force-field generator. The shape of the field is determined by guides made of a special alloy. The field is so small you couldn't see it, even if it was visible, which it isn't, with nine electron microscopes in series. But that blue wire around the edge is so composed that every atom in it is an exact analog of the subatomic particles forming the guides. And for reasons of spatial stress that I won't waste your time with, an analog of the field appears inside the loop. Right? Right. That's the gadget, the building block. Everything else around here is done by piling it up. The window—that's an analog loop. There's two of 'em holding up this building—you didn't think it was done with prayer, did you?"

"The building? But—the spoon was a loop, and I imagine the window is too, but I don't see any loops outside the building. It would have to be outside, wouldn't it?"

"It sure would. You have an eye, but you don't need an eye to see that. Sure, this heap is propped up two ways from the outside. And the loops *are* there. But instead of being made of alloy, they're standing waves. If you don't know what a standing wave is I won't bother you with it. See that?" He pointed.

Charlie followed his fingers and saw the ruins and the great strangler fig.

"That," said Seace, "is one of the props, or the outer end of it. Try to imagine a model of this building, held up by two triangles of transparent plastic, and you'll have an idea of the shape and size of the fields."

"What happens when somebody walks into it?"

"Nobody does. Cut an arch in the ground-line of your piece of plastic, and you'll see why not. Sometimes a bird hits one, poor thing, but mostly they seem to be able to avoid it. It remains invisible because the surface isn't really a surface, but a vibrating matrix of forces, and dust won't sit on it. And it's perfectly transparent."

"But . . . doesn't it yield? The bowl of that spoon I used, it sagged under the weight of the food—I saw it. And these windows . . ."

"You *have* got an eye!" Seace commended. "Well, wood is matter, brick is matter, steel is matter. What's the difference between them? Why, what's in 'em, and how it's put together, that's all. The A-field can be dialled to be anything you want it to be—thick, thin, impermeable, what have you. Also rigid—rigid like nothing else has ever been."

Charlie thought: That's just dandy as long as you pay your electric bill to keep the thing up there; but he didn't say it because the language had no word for "electric bill," or even "pay."

He looked out at the strangler fig, squinted his eyes, and tried to see the thing that was holding the building up. "I bet you can see it when it rains," he said at last.

"No you can't," said Seace briskly. "Doesn't rain."

Charlie looked up at the bright overcast. "What?"

Seace joined him and also looked up. "You're looking at the underside of an A-field bubble."

"You mean—"

"Sure, all of Ledom is under a roof. Temperature controlled, humidity controlled, breezes blowing when they're told to."

"And no night . . ."

"We don't sleep, so why bother?"

Charlie had heard that sleep was quite possibly an inbred tendency, inherited from cave-folk who of necessity crouched unmoving in caves during dark hours to avoid the nocturnal carnivore; according to the theory, the ability to lose consciousness and relax during those times became a survival factor.

He glanced again at the sky. "What's outside, Seace?"

"Better leave that to Philos."

Charlie began to grin, and then the smile cut off. This shunting from one expert to another seemed always to occur when he skirted the matter of the end of the human species as he had known it.

"Just tell me one thing, as—ah—a matter of theory, Seace. If the A-field is transparent to light, it would be transparent to any radiation, no?"

"No," said Seace. "I told you—it's what we dial it up to be, including opaque."

"Oh," said Charlie. He turned his eyes away from the sky, and he sighed.

"So much for static effects," said Seace briskly. Charlie appreciated his understanding. "Now: the dynamic. I told you, this stuff can do anything the electric motor and electricity can do. Want to move earth? Dial an analog field down so thin it'll slip between molecules, slide it into a hillside. Expand it a few millimeters, back it out. Out comes a shovel full—but the shovel is as big as you want it to be, and your analog can be floated anywhere you want it. Anything can be handled that way. One man can create and control forms for pouring foundations and walls, for example, remove them by causing them to cease to exist. And it isn't any sand-and-chemical mud you pour; the A-field can homogenize and realign practically anything." He thumped the concrete-like curved pillar at the side of the window.

Charlie, who at one time had run a bulldozer, began to compliment himself on his early determination to be only impressed, but not amazed, by technology. He recalled one time on a drydock job, when he was driving an Allis-Chalmers HD-14 angledozer back to the tractor shop to have a new corner welded on the blade, and a labor foreman flagged him and asked him to backfill a trench. While the pick-and-shovel boys scrambled out of the way, he backfilled and tamped a hundred feet of trench on one pass, in about 90 seconds—a job which would have taken the 60-odd men the rest of the week. Given the gadgetry, one skilled man is a hundred, a thousand, ten thousand. It was difficult, but not impossible, to visualize the likes of the Medical One, four hundred feet high, being put up in a week by three men.

"And more on the dynamic side. The right A-field can make like an X-ray for such things as cancer control and genetic mutation effects—but without burns or other side effects. I suppose you've noticed all the new plants?"

All the new people too, said Charlie, but not aloud.

"That grass out there. Nobody mows it; it just lies there. With the A-field we transport everything and anything, process food, manufacture fabrics—oh everything; and the power consumption is really negligible."

"What kind of power is it?"

Seace pulled at his horse-nostrilled nose. "Ever hear of negative matter?"

"Is that the same thing as contraterrene matter—where the electron has a positive charge and the nucleus is negative?"

"You surprise me! I didn't know you people had come so far."

"Some guys who wrote science fiction stories came that far."

"Right. Now, know what happens if negative matter comes in contact with normal matter?"

"Blam. The biggest kind."

"That's right—all the mass turns into energy, and with the tiniest particle of mass, that still turns out to be a whole *lot* of energy. Now: the A-field can construct an analog of anything—even a small mass of negative matter. It's quite good enough to make a transformation with normal matter and release energy—all you want. So—you construct the analog field with an electrical exciter. When it begins to yield, a very simple feedback makes it maintain itself, with plenty of energy left over to do work."

"I don't pretend to understand it," smiled Charlie. "I just believe it."

Seace smiled back, and said with mock severity, "You came here to discuss science, not religion." Brisk again, he went on, "Let's call it quits on the A-field, then, right? Right. All I really wanted to point out to you was that it is, in itself, simple, and that it can do almost anything. I said earlier—or if I didn't I meant to—that all of Ledom has, as keystones, two simple things, and that's one of them. The other—the other has the made-up name of cerebrostyle."

"Let me guess." He translated the term into English and was going to say, "A new fashion in brains?" but the gag wouldn't take in Ledom: "Style" was indeed a word and concept in Ledom, but it was not the same word as the suffix (in Ledom) of "cerebrostyle." This second kind of style had the feeling of *stylus*, or writing implement. "Something to write on brains with."

"You've got the point," said Seace, "but not by the handle. . . . It's something a brain writes on. Well . . . put it this way. Being impressed by a brain is its first function. And it can be used—and it is used—to impress things on brains."

Confused, Charlie smiled, "You'd better tell me what it is, first."

"Just a little colloidal matter in a box. That, of course, is an over-simplification. And to continue the mistake of over-simplifying, what it does when it's hooked up to a brain is to make a synaptic record of any particular sequence that brain is performing. You probably know enough about the learning process to know that a mere statement of the conclusion is never enough to teach anything. To the untaught mind, my statement that alcohol and water inter-penetrate on the molecular level might be taken on faith, but not in any other way. But if I lead up to it, demonstrate by measuring out a quantity of each, and mixing them, show that the result is less than twice the original measure, it begins to make some sense. And to go back even further, before that makes any sense, I must be sure that the learning mind is equipped with the concepts 'alcohol,' 'water,' 'measure,' and 'mix,' and further that it is contrary to the brand of ignorance known as common sense that equal quantities of two fluids should aggregate to less than twice the original amount. In other words, each conclusion must be preceded by a logical and consistent series, all based on previous observation and proof.

"And what the cerebrostyle does is to absorb certain sequences from, say, my mind and then transfers them to, say, yours; but it is not the mere presentation of a total, a conclusion; it is the instillation of the entire sequence which led up to it. It's done almost instantaneously, and all that's required of the receiving mind is to correlate it with what's already there. That last, incidentally, is a full-time job."

"I'm not sure that I—" Charlie wavered.

Seace drove on. "What I mean is that if, among a good many proven data, the mind contained some logically-arrived-at statement—and mind you, logic and truth are two totally different things—to the effect that alcohol and water are immiscible—that statement would ultimately find itself in conflict with other statements. Which one would win out would depend on how much true and demonstrable data were there to match it against. At length (actually, damn soon) the mind would determine that one of the statements was wrong. That situation will itch until the mind finds out *why* it's wrong—that is, until it has exhaustively compared each logical step, from premise to conclusion, of every relative step of every other conclusion."

"A pretty fair teaching device."

"It's the only known substitute for experience," smiled Seace, "and a sight faster. I want to stress the fact that this isn't just indoctrination. It would be impossible to impress untruth on a mind with the cerebrostyle, however logical, because sooner or later a conclusion would be presented which was contrary to the observed facts, and the whole thing would fall apart. And likewise, the cerebrostyle is not a sort of 'mind probe' designed to dig out your inner secrets. We have been able to distinguish between the dynamic, or sequence-in-action currents of the mind, and the static, or storage parts. If a teacher records the alcohol-and-water sequence to its conclusion, the student is not going to get the teacher's life-history and tastes in fruit along with his lesson in physics.

"I wanted you to understand this because you'll be going out among the people soon and you'll probably wonder where they get their education. Well, they get it from the cerebrostyle, in half-hour sessions once each twenty-eight days. And you may take my word for it, for every other of those days they are working full time on the correlations—no matter what else they may be doing."

"I'd like a look at that gadget."

"I haven't one here, but you've already met it. How else do you suppose you learned an entire language in—oh, I guess it was all of twelve minutes?"

"That hood thing in the operating room behind Mielwis' office!"

"That's right."

Charlie thought that over for a moment, and then said, "Seace, if you can do that, what's all this nonsense about having me learn all I can about Ledom before you'll send me home? Why not just cook my head under that thing for another twelve minutes and give it to me that way?"

Seace shook his head gravely. "It's your opinion we want. *Your* opinion, Charlie Johns. The one thing the cerebrostyle gives you is the truth, and when you get it, you *know* it's the truth. We want you to get your information through the instrument known as Charlie Johns, to learn the conclusions of that Charlie Johns."

"I think you mean I'm not going to believe some of the things I see."

"I know you're not. You see? The cerebrostyle would give us Charlie Johns' reaction to the truth. Your own observations will give us Charlie Johns' reaction to what he thinks is the truth."

"And why is that so important to you?"

Seace spread his cool clever hands. "We take a bearing. Check our course." And before Charlie could evaluate that, or question him further, he hurried to sum up:

"So you see we aren't miracle-workers, magicians. And don't be surprised to find out that we're not, after all, primarily a technological culture. We can do a great deal, true. But we do it with only two devices which, as far as Philos is able to tell me, are unfamiliar to you—the A-field and the cerebrostyle. With them we can eliminate power—both man- and machine-power—as a problem; we have more than we'll ever need. And what you would call education no longer takes appreciable power or plant or personnel, or time.

Likewise, we have no shortages of food, housing, or clothing. All of which leaves the people free for other things."

Charlie asked, "What other things, for God's sake?"

Seace smiled. "You'll see . . ."

"**M**OMMY?" KAREN DEMANDS. JEANETTE IS GIVING THE three-year-old her bath.

"Yes, honey."

"Did I reely reely come out of your tummy?"

"Yes, honey."

"No I didn't."

"Who says you didn't?"

"Davy says *he* came out of your tummy."

"Well, he did. Close your eyes tight-tight-tight or you'll get soap in 'em."

"Well if Davy came out of your tummy why didn't I come out of Daddy's tummy?"

Jeanette bites her lip—she always tries her best not to laugh at her children unless they are laughing first—and applies shampoo.

"Well Mommy, *why*?"

"Only Mommies get babies in their tummies, honey."

"Not daddies, ever?"

"Not ever."

Jeanette sudses and rinses and sudses again and rinses again, and nothing more is said until the pink little face safely regains its wide-open blue eyes. "I want bubbles."

"Oh *honey!* Your hair's all rinsed!" But the pleading look, the I'm-trying-not-to-cry look, conquers, and she smiles and relents. "All right, just for a while, Karen. But mind, don't get bubbles on your hair. All right?"

"Right." Karen watches gleefully as Jeanette pours a packet of bubble-bath into the water and turns on the hot faucet. Jeanette stands by, partly to guard the hair, partly because she enjoys it. "Well then," says Karen abruptly, "we don't need daddies then."

"Whatever do you mean? Who would go to the office and bring back lollipops and lawnmowers and everything?"

"Not for that. I mean for babies. Daddies can't make babies."

"Well, darling, they *help*."

"How, Mommy?"

"That's enough bubbles. The water's getting too hot." She shuts off the water.

"*How*, Mommy?"

"Well, darling, it's a little hard maybe for you to understand, but what happens is that a daddy has a very special kind of loving. It's very wonderful and beautiful, and when he loves a mommy like that, very very much, she can have a baby."

While she is talking, Karen has found a flat sliver of soap and is trying to see if it fits. Jeanette reaches down into the bathwater and snatches her hand up and slaps it. "Karen! Don't touch yourself *down there*. It's not *nice!*"

"Getting the hang of it?"

Charlie glanced thoughtfully at Philos, who had been waiting for him at the foot of the invisible lift, as always appearing as if he just happened to be there, as always with the alert dark eyes sparkling with some secret amusement . . . or perhaps just knowledge . . . or perhaps something quite different, like grief. "Seace," said Charlie, "has the darndest way of answering every question you ask, and leaving you with the feeling he's concealing something."

Philos laughed. As Charlie has noticed before, Philos had a good laugh. "I guess," said the Ledom, "you're ready for the main part of it. The Children's One."

Charlie looked across at the Medical One, and up at the Science One. "These are pretty 'main,' I'd say."

"No they're not," said Philos positively. "They're the parameters, if you like—the framework, the mechanical pulse, but for all that they're only the outer edge, and a thin one at that. The Children's One is the biggest of all."

Charlie looked up at the tilting bulk over him and marveled. "It must be a long way from here."

"Why do you say that?"

"Anything bigger than this—"

"—you'd see from here? Well, there it is." Philos pointed—

—at a cottage. It lay in a fold of the hills, surrounded by that impeccable greensward, and up its white, low walls, flaming flowering vines grew. Its roof was pitched and gabled, brown with a dusting of green. There were flower-boxes at the windows, and at one end, the white wall yielded to the charm of fieldstone, tapering up to be a chimney, from which blue smoke drifted.

"Mind walking that far?"

Charlie sniffed the warm bright air, and felt the green springiness under his feet. "Mind!"

They walked toward the distant cottage, taking a winding course through the gently rolling land. Once Charlie said, "Just that?"

"You'll see," said Philos. He seemed taut with expectancy and delight. "Have you ever had any children?"

"No," said Charlie, and thought immediately of Laura.

"If you had," said Philos, "would you love them?"

"Well, I guess I would!"

"Why?" Philos demanded. Then he stopped and with great gravity took Charlie's arm and turned him to face him, and said slowly, "Don't answer that question. Just think about it."

Startled, Charlie could think of no response except, at last, "All right," which Philos accepted. They walked on. The sense of expectancy somehow increased. It was Philos, of course; the Ledom radiated something. . . . Charlie remembered having seen a movie once, a sort of travelogue. The camera was placed on an airplane which flew low over plains country, over houses and fields, with the near land rushing past, and the musical background was as expectant as this. The film gave you no warning of the absolute enormity that was to come; for time and distance which seemed forever, there was only the flat country and the speed, and the occasional road and farm, but the music grew in tension and suspense, until with an absolute explosion of color and of perspective, you found yourself hurtling over the lip of the Grand Canyon of the Colorado.

"Look there," said Philos.

Charlie looked, and saw a young Ledom in a yellow silken tunic, leaning against a rocky outcropping in a steep bank not far ahead. As they approached, Charlie expected anything but what actually happened; when one meets a fellow being, there is reaction, interaction of some kind, whether one is homo sap. or Ledom or beaver; but here there was none. The Ledom in yellow stood on one leg, back against the rock, one foot against the other knee, both hands clasped under the raised thigh. The rather fine-drawn face was averted, turned neither directly toward them nor away, and the eyes were half-closed.

Charlie said in a low voice, "What's—"

"Shh!" hissed Philos.

They walked unhurriedly past the standing figure. Philos veered close and signalling to Charlie to be silent, passed a hand back and forth close to the half-closed eyes. There was no response.

Philos and Charlie walked on, Charlie turning frequently to look back. All the while they were in sight, there was no movement but the gentle shifting of the silken garment in the light breeze. When at last a turn put a shoulder of the hill between them and the entranced creature, Charlie said, "I thought you said the Ledom don't sleep."

"That isn't sleep."

"It'll do until the real thing comes along. Or is he sick?"

"Oh no! . . . I'm glad you saw that. You'll see it again, here and there. He's just—stopped."

"But what's the matter with him?"

"Nothing, I tell you. It's a—well, call it a pause. It was not uncommon in your time. Your American Indians, the Plains Indians, could do it. So could some of the Atlas Mountain nomads. It isn't sleep. It's something that, doubtless, you do when you sleep. Did you ever study sleep?"

"Not what you might call study."

"I have," said Philos. "One thing of especial interest is that when you sleep, you dream. Actually, you hallucinate. Sleeping regularly as you do, you perform this hallucination while you are sleeping, although sleep is here, as in many other ways, only a convenience; even you can do it without sleeping."

"Well, there's what we called daydreaming—"

"Whatever you call it, it's a phenomenon universal to the human mind, and perhaps I shouldn't limit it to humanity. Anyway, the fact remains that if the mind is inhibited, or prohibited, from performing the hallucinations, for example by being wakened each time it slips into this state, it breaks down."

"The mind breaks down?"

"That's right."

"You mean if you had wakened that Ledom there, he'd have gone insane?" Brutally he demanded, "Are you all that delicately balanced?"

Philos laughed away the brutality; it was a sincere response to something ludicrous. "No! Oh, never that! I was talking about a laboratory situation, a constant and relentless interruption. I can assure you that he saw us; he was aware. But his mind made a choice, and chose to pursue whatever it was that was going on in his head. If I had persisted, or if something so unusual as the sound of *your* voice"—the emphasis was slight but meaningful; it occurred then to Charlie that his voice here was a baritone horn among flutes—"had snapped him out of it, he would have talked normally with us, forgiven us for the intrusion, waved us good-bye."

"But why do it? What does he do it *for*?"

"What do you do it for? . . . It seems to be a mechanism by which the mind detaches itself from reality in order to compare and relate data which in reality cannot be associated. Your literature is full of hallucinatory images of the sort—pigs with wings, human freedom, fire-breathing dragons, the wisdom of the majority, the basilisk, the *golem*, and equality of the sexes.

"Now look—" Charlie cried angrily, and then checked himself. The likes of Philos could not be reached by rage; he sensed that, and said bluntly, "You're playing with me, so it's a game. But you know the rules and I don't."

Disarmingly, Philos cut it out, then and there; his sharp eyes softened and in complete sincerity, he apologized. "I'm previous," he added. "My turn comes after you've seen the rest of Ledom."

"Your turn?"

"Yes—the history. What you think of Ledom is one thing; what you will think of Ledom plus its history is another; what you will—but never mind that."

"You'd better go on."

"I was going to say, what you will think of Ledom plus its history plus *your* history is another matter altogether. But I won't say it," declared Philos engagingly, "because if I did I should only have to apologize again."

In spite of himself Charlie laughed with him, and they went on.

A few hundred yards from the cottage, Philos turned him sharp right and they climbed a rather steep slope to its crest, and followed it until they came to a knoll. Philos, in the lead, stopped and waved Charlie up beside him. "Let's watch them for a little while."

Charlie found himself looking down on the cottage. He could now see that it was at the brink of a wide valley, part wooded (or was that orchard? They *wouldn't* do anything in straight lines here!) and part cultivated fields. Around and between the fields and woods, the country was as parklike as it had been by the big buildings. Scattered throughout were more cottages, widely separated, each unique—timber, fieldstone, a sort of white stucco, plaster, even what looked like turf—and each widely separated from all the others, some by as much as half a mile. He could see more than twenty-five of the cottages from their vantage point, and there were probably more. Like scattered, diverse flower-petals, the bright garments of the people showed here and there through the woods and fields, on the green borders, and on the banks of the two small streams which wandered down the valley. The silver sky domed it all, falling to hills all about; it seemed then to be a dish-shaped mesa, and higher than anything around it, for he could see nothing beyond the gentle ramparts of the valley itself.

"The Children's One," said Philos.

Charlie looked down past the growing thatch of the cottage below, to the yard and pond before it. He began to hear the singing, and he saw the children.

MR. AND MRS. HERBERT RAILE ARE SHOPPING FOR CHILDREN'S clothes in the dry-goods wing of an enormous highway supermarket. The children are outside in the car. It is hot out there so they are hurrying. Herb pushes a supermarket shopping cart. Jeanette fans through the stacks of clothes on the counters.

"Oh, look! Little T-shirts! Just like the real thing." She takes three for Davy, size Five, and three for Karen, size Three, and drops them in the cart. "Now, pants."

She marches briskly off, with Herb and the shopping cart in her wake. He unthinkingly follows the international rules of the road: a vessel approaching from the right has the right of way; a vessel making a turn loses the right of way. He yields right of way twice on these principles and has to run to catch up. A wheel squeaks. When he runs it screams. Jeanette proceeds purposively right, straight ahead three aisles, and left two, and then stops dead. A little breathless, Herb and squeak regain her aura.

She demands, "Now where are pants?"

He points. "Over there where it says PANTS." They had early passed within an aisle of it. Jeanette *tsks* in her haste and retraces her quick steps. Herb wheels and squeaks after her.

"Corduroy too hot. All the Graham kids in denim right now. You know Louie Graham didn't get his promotion," murmurs Jeanette like one in prayer, and passes up the denim. "Khaki. Here we are. Size Five." She takes two pairs. "Size Three." She takes two pairs, and drops them into the cart, and hurries off. Herb squeaks, stops, screams, and squeaks after her. She takes two turns left, proceeds three aisles and stops. "Where are children's sandals?"

"Over there where it says CHILDREN'S SANDALS," pants Herb, pointing. Jeanette *tsks,* and sprints to the sandals. By the time he overtakes her she has picked out two pairs of red sandals with yellow-white gum soles, and drops them into the cart.

"*Stop!*" gurgles Herb, almost laughing.

"What is it?" she says in midstride.

"What do you want now?"

"Bathing suits."

"Well look there then, where it says BATHING SUITS."

"Don't nag, dear," she says, moving off.

He maneuvers a stretch in which, briefly, he can wheel beside her close enough to be heard over the squeaks, and says, "The difference between men and women is—"

"A dollar ninety-seven," she says, passing a counter.

"—that men read directions and women don't. I think it's a matter of sexual pride. Take some out-and-out-genius of a packager, he dreams up a box for you to pinch it, tear back to dotted line, and then gives you a string to pull open the inner liner."

"Leotards," she says, passing a counter.

"Nine engineers bust their brains on the packaging machinery. Sixteen buyers go out of their heads finding enough of the right materials. Twenty-three traffic men answer two A.M. phone calls moving seventy thousand tons of material. And when you get it into your kitchen you open it with a ham slicer."

"Bathing suits," she says. "What did you say, honey?"

"Nothing, honey."

She rapidly scatters the contents of a bin called *Size 5.* "Here we are." She holds up a small pair of trunks, navy with red piping.

"Looks like a diaper."

"It stretches," she says; perhaps this is a *sequitur* but he does not investigate. He rummages through *Size 3* and comes up with a similar pair of trunks, but about as large as his palm. "Here it is. Let's beat it before those kids fry out there."

"Oh *Herb!* silly: that's a *boy's* bathing suit!"

"I think it would look cute as hell on Karen."

"But Herb! It hasn't any *top!*" she cries, rummaging.

He holds up the little trunks and looks ruminatively at them. "What does Karen need a top for? Three years old!"

"Here's one. Oh dear, it's the same as Dolly Graham's."

"Is there anybody in our neighborhood who is going to be aroused at the sight of a three-year-old's tit?"

"Herb, don't talk dirty."

"I don't like the implication."

"*Here* we are!" She displays her find and giggles. "Oh, how very, very *sweet!*" She drops it into the shopping cart, and they squeak swiftly toward the checkout, with their six T-shirts, four khaki shorts, two pairs of red sandals with yellow-white gum soles, one size 5 navy swimming trunks, one size 3 perfect miniature bikini.

*T*he children, more than a dozen of them, were in and around the pond, and as they played, they sang.

Charlie had never heard such singing. He had heard much worse, and, as singing goes, some better; but he had never heard singing *like* this. It was something like the soft sound made by one of those tops which gives out an organ-toned chord, and then, slowing, shifts to another, related chord. Sometimes such toys are designed to issue a single constant note, which sounds as part of the two or even three chords as they modulate. These children, some in adolescence, some mere toddlers, sang that way; and the extraordinary thing about it was that, of the fifteen or so voices which at one time or another involved themselves, never more than four, or very occasionally five, sang at once. The chord of music hung over the group, sometimes bunched over a cluster of small brown bodies, then moving by degrees across the pond to the other side, then spreading itself out so that alto notes came from the left, soprano from the right. One could almost watch the chord as it condensed, rarefied, hovered, spread, leapt, changing its hues all the while in compelling sequences, tonic, then holding the keynote reinforced by two voices in unison while the background shifted to make it a dominant, one fell away to a seventh, and then, rather than drop back to the tonic, one voice would flat a halftone and the chord, turned blue, would float there as the relative minor. Then a fifth, a sixth, a ninth sweet discord and it would right itself as the tonic chord in another key—all so easy, so true and sweet.

Most of the children were naked; all were straight-limbed, clear-eyed, firm-bodied. To Charlie's as yet uneducated eye they all looked like little girls. They seemed not to concentrate at all on their music; they played, splashed, ran about, built with mud and sticks and colored bricks; three of them threw a ball amongst them. They spoke to each other in their dove-like language, called, squeaked as they ran and were almost caught, squealed too, and one cried like—well, like a child, when he fell (and was ever so quickly caught up by three others, comforted, kissed, given a toy, teased to laughter) but over it all hung that changing three-part, four-part, sometimes five-part chord, built by one and another in a pause, between breaths, in midair diving into the water, between spoken question and answer. Charlie had heard something like this before, in the central court of the Medical One, but not so bright, so easy; and he was to hear this chordal music wherever he went in Ledom, wherever the Ledom gathered in larger groups; it hung over the Ledom as the fog of their body-heat hangs over the reindeer herds in the frigid Lapland plains.

"Why do they sing like that?"

"They do everything together," said Philos, eyes shining. "And when they're together, doing different things, they do that. They can be together, feel together, singing like that no matter what else they may be doing. They feel it, like the light of the sky on their backs, without thinking about it, just—loving it. They change it for the pleasure of it, the way that one walks from the cold water to the warm stones, for the feeling on his feet. They keep it in the air, they take it from the air around them and give it back. Here, let me show you something." Softly, but clearly, he sang three notes rapidly: *do, sol, mi* . . .

And as if the notes were bright play-bullets, shot to each of three children, three children picked them up—one child for each note, so that the notes come in as arpeggio and were held as chord; then they were repeated, again as arpeggio and again held; and now one child—Charlie saw which one, too; it was one standing waist-deep in the pond—changed one note, so that the arpeggio was *do, fa mi* . . . and immediately afterward *re, fa mi*, and suddenly *fa, do la* . . . so it went, progressing, modulating, inverting; augmented, with sixths added, with ninths added, with demanding sevenths asking the tonic but mischievously getting the related minor instead. At length the arpeggio was lost as an arpeggio, and the music eased itself back to a steady, constantly changing chord.

"That's . . . just beautiful," breathed Charlie, wishing he could say it as beautifully as the beauty he heard, and disliking himself for his inability.

Philos said, gladly, "There's Grocid!"

Grocid, a scarlet cloak ribboned about his throat, the rest of it airborne, had just emerged from the cottage. He turned and looked up, waved and sang the three notes Philos had sung (and again they were caught, braided, turned and tossed among the children) and laughed.

Philos said to Charlie, "He's saying that he knew who it was the instant he heard those notes." He called, "Grocid! May we come?"

Grocid gladly waved them in, and they plunged down the steep slope. Grocid snatched up a child and came to meet them. The child sat astride his shoulders, crowing with joy and batting at the billows on the cloak. "Ah, Philos. You've brought Charlie Johns. Come down, come down! It's good to see you." To Charlie's astonishment, Grocid and Philos kissed. When Grocid approached him, Charlie stiffly stuck out his hand; with instant understanding, Grocid took it, pressed it, let it go. "This is Anaw," said Grocid, brushing the side of the child's cheek with his hair. The youngster laughed, buried its face in the thick mass, extricated a laughing eye, and with it peeped at Charlie. Charlie laughed back.

They went together into the house. Dilating bulkheads? Concealed lighting? Anti-gravity tea-trays? Self-frosting breakfast food? Automatic floors?

No.

The room was near enough to being rectangular as it needed to be to satisfy eyes which had become, Charlie suddenly realized, hungry for a straight line. The ceiling was low and raftered, and it was cool there—not the antiseptic and unemotional kiss of conditioned air, but the coolness of vine-awninged windows, low ceilings, and thick walls; it was the natural seepage of the earth itself's cool subcutaneous layers. And here were chairs—one of hand-rubbed wood, three of rustic design, with curves of tough liana and slats and spokes of whole or split tree-trunks. The floor was flagstone, levelled and ground smooth and grouted with, of all things, a glazed purple cement, and brilliant hand-tied rag rugs set it off. On a low table was a gigantic wooden bowl, turned from a single piece of hardwood, and a graceful but very rugged beverage set—a pitcher and seven or eight earthenware mugs. In the bowl was a salad, beautifully arranged in an elaborate star-pattern, of fruits, nuts, and vegetables.

There were pictures on the walls, mostly in true-earth colors—greens, browns, orange, and the yellow-tinted reds and red-tinted blues of flowers and ripe fruit. Most were representational and pleasingly so; some were abstract, a few impressionistic. One especially caught his eye; a scene of two Ledom, with the observation angle strangely high and askew, so that you seemed to be looking down past the shoulder of the standing figure to the reclining one below. The latter seemed to be broken in some unspecified way, ill and in pain; the whole composition was oddly blurred, and its instant impact was of being seen through scalding tears.

"I'm very glad you could come." It was the other head of the Children's One, Nasive, standing by him and smiling. Charlie turned away from his contemplation of the picture and saw the Ledom, in a cloak exactly the same as Grocid's, extending his hand. Charlie shook it and let it slip away; he said, "I am too. I like it here."

"We rather thought you would," said Nasive. "Not too different from what you're used to, I'll bet."

Charlie could have nodded and let it go, but in this place, with these people, he wanted to be honest. "Too different from most of what I've been used to," he said. "We had some of this, here and there. Not enough of it."

"Sit down. We'll have a bite now—just to keep us going. Leave some room, though; we'll be in on a real feast shortly."

Grocid filled all-but-rimless earthenware plates and passed them around, while Nasive poured a golden liquid into the mugs. It was,

Charlie discovered, a sharp but honey-flavored beverage, probably a sort of mead, cool but not cold, with a spicy aftertaste and a late, gentle kick. The salad, which he ate with a satin-finished hardwood fork which had two short, narrow tines and one broad long one with a very adequate cutting edge, was eleven ways delicious (one for each variety of food it contained) and it strained his self-control to the utmost not to *a*) gobble and *b*) demand more.

They talked; he did not join in very much, although aware of their courteous care to say that which might include or interest him, or at least not to launch into anything of length which might exclude him. Fredon had weevils over the hill there. Have you seen the new inlay process Dregg's doing? Wood in ceramic; you'd swear they'd been fireglazed together. Nariah wanted to put in for biostatic treatment of a new milkweed fiber. Eriu's kid broke his silly leg. And meanwhile the children were in and out, miraculously never actually interrupting, but simply flashing in, receiving a nut or a piece of fruit, hovering breathlessly to ask a favor, a permission, or a fact: "Illew says a dragonfly is a kind of spider. Is it?" (No; none of the arachnids have wings.) A flash of purple ribbon and yellow tunic, and the child is gone, to be replaced instantly by a very small and coquettish naked creature which said clearly, "Grocid, you got a funny face." (You got a funny face too.) Laughing, the mite was gone.

Charlie, eating with effortful slowness, watched Nasive, crouched on a nearby hassock, deftly prying a splinter out of his own hand. The hand, though graceful, was large and strong, and seeing the point of a needle-like probe excavating below the base of the middle finger, Charlie was struck by the sight of the callosities there. The flesh of the palm and the inside of the fingers seemed as tough as a stevedore's. Charlie found himself making an effort to square this with flowing scarlet garments and "art" furniture, and realized it wasn't his privilege, just now, to draw such balances. But he said, thumping the sturdy arm of the rustic chair, "Are these made here?"

"*Right* here," said Nasive cheerfully. "Made it myself. Grocid and I did this whole place. With the kids, of course. Grocid made the plates and the mugs. Like 'em?"

"I really do," said Charlie. They were brown and almost gold, swirled together. "Is it a lacquer on earthware, or is that A-field of yours a kiln for you?"

"Neither," said Nasive. "Would you like to see how we do it?" He glanced at Charlie's empty plate. "Or would you like some—"

Regretfully, Charlie laid the plate aside. "I'd like to see that."

They rose and went toward a door at the back. A child half-hidden in the drapes at the back of the room darted mischievously at Nasive, who, without breaking stride, caught it up, turned it squealing upside down, very gently bumped its head on the floor, and set it on its feet again. Then grinning, he waved Charlie through the door.

"You're very fond of children," said Charlie.

"My God," said Nasive.

And here again the language was shaded so that a translation must lose substance. Charlie felt that what he meant when he said "My God" was a direct response to his remark, and in no sense an expletive. Was the child his God, then? Or . . . was it the concept The Child?

The room in which they stood was a little higher than the one they had left, and wider, but utterly different from the harmonious, casual, comfortable living space. This was a workshop—a real working workshop. The floor was brick, the walls were planed but otherwise unfinished planks, milled shiplap fashion. On wooden pegs hung tools, basic tools: sledge and wedges, hammers, adze, spoke-shave, awl, draw-knife, hatchet and axe, square, gauge, and levels, brace and a rack of bits, and a set of planes. Against the walls, and here and there out on the floor, were—well, call them machine tools, but they were apparently hand-fashioned, sometimes massively, from wood! A tablesaw, for example, was powered from underneath by treadles, and by a crank and connecting rod arrangement, caused a sort of sabresaw to oscillate up and down. A detachable, deep-throated frame was clamped to it, to guide the top end of the saw-blade, and was loaded with a *wooden* spring.

There was a lathe, too, with clusters of wooden pulleys for speed adjustment, and an immense flywheel—it must have weighed five hundred pounds—made of ceramic.

But it was the kiln which Nasive had brought him to see. It stood in the corner, a brick construction with a chimney above and a heavy metal door, which stood up on brick pilings. Underneath was a firepot on casters—"it's our forge, too," Nasive pointed out as, with a muscular tug, he rolled it out and back under again—and mounted on it, well to one side, was a treadle-operated bellows. The outlet from the bellows led to a great floppy object which looked like a deflated bladder, which in fact it was. Nasive pumped vigorously on the treadle and the wrinkled thing sighed, tiredly got up off its back, and wobbled upright. It then began to swell.

"I got the idea from a bagpipe one of the kids was learning to play," said Nasive, his face glowing. He stopped pumping and pulled a lever a little way toward him; Charlie heard air hissing up through the grates. He pulled it a bit more, and the air roared. "You have all the control you could possibly want and you don't have to tell some brawny adult to take a long trick at it; all the kids in the place can come in and each does as much as he can, even the little ones. They love it."

"That's wonderful," said Charlie sincerely, "but—surely there's an easier way to do it."

"Oh, surely," said Nasive agreeably—and not by one word did he enlarge on it.

Charlie looked admiringly about him, at the neat stacks of lumber which had obviously been milled here, the sturdy bracing of the wooden machines, the—"Look here," said Nasive. He threw a clamp from the chuck end of the lathe ways and gave the ways a shove upward. Hinged at the tailstock end, it swung upright and latched into place—"A drill press!" cried Charlie, delighted.

He pointed to the flywheel. "That looks like ceramic. How did you ever fire anything that size?"

Nasive nodded toward the kiln. "It'll take it. Just barely. Of course, it was in there for a while . . . we had to clear out the rest of the place and hold a feast and dancing until it was done."

"With the people dancing on the treadle," laughed Charlie.

"And everywhere else. It was quite a party," Nasive laughed back. "But you wanted to know why we made the flywheel of ceramic. Well, it's massive, and it was less work to cast it to run true than it would be to true up a stone one."

"I don't doubt that," said Charlie, looking at the flywheel but thinking of invisible elevators, time machines, a fingertip device which, he had been told, could take large bites out of hillsides and transport what it bit wherever it was wanted. The fleeting thought occurred to him that perhaps these people out here didn't know what they had back at the big Ones. Then he recalled that it was at the Medical One he had first seen Grocid and Nasive. So then the thought came to him that, knowing what they had at the Ones, they were denied these things, and must plod from cottage to field, and work up those case-hardened callouses, while Seace and Mielwis magicked ice-cold breakfast fruits from holes in the wall by their beds. Ah well. Them as has, gits. "Anyway, that is really one large hunk of ceramic."

"Oh, not really," said Nasive. "Come and look."

He led the way to a door in the outside wall, and they stepped through into a garden. Four or five of the children were tumbling about on the grass, and one was up a tree. They shouted, cooed, crowed at the sight of Nasive, flew to him and away; while he talked he would tousle one, spin another around, answer a third with a wink and a tickle.

Charlie Johns saw the statue.

He thought, would you call this Madonna and Child?

The adult figure, with some material that draped like fine linen thrown loosely half around it, knelt, looking upward. The figure of the child stood, also looking upward, with a transcendent, even ecstatic expression on its face. The child was nude, but its flesh tones were perfectly reproduced, as were the adult's, whose garment was shot through with all colors possible to a wood fire.

The two remarkable features about this sculpture were, first, that the figure of the adult was three feet high, and that of the child over *eleven feet*!; second, that the entire group was one monstrous single piece of perfectly glazed, faultlessly fired terra cotta.

Charlie had to ask Nasive to repeat himself, saying something about kilns, as he was swept with wonderment at the beauty of this work of art, its finish, but most of all its symbolism. The small adult kneeling in worship of the giant child, rapt face fixed on the huge standing figure; and the child, in a rapture of its own, detached from the adult and aspiring upward . . . somewhere . . . higher in any case.

"*That* kiln I can't show you," Nasive was saying.

Charlie, still spellbound, scanned the great lovely work, wondering if it had been fired in pieces and erected. But no; the glaze was flawless, without line or join from top to bottom. Why, even the base, made and colored like a great mass of flowers, a regular mound of petals, was glazed!

Well then! They did get a crack at that A-field magic after all!

Nasive said, "It was sculpted right where it stands, and fired there too. Grocid and I did most of it, except the flowers; the children did the flowers. More than two hundred children screened all that clay, and worked it so it wouldn't fracture in the fire."

"Oh . . . and you built your kiln around it!"

"We built three kilns around it—one to dry it, which we tore down so we could paint it; one to set the color glazes, which we tore down to coat it, and one for the final glaze."

"Which you tore down and threw away."

"We didn't throw it away. We used the bricks for the new floor in the workshop. But even if we had thrown it away—it was worth it."

"It was worth it," said Charlie. "Nasive . . . what *is* it? What does it mean?"

"It's called The Maker," said Nasive. (In the language, that was *creator*, and also *the one who accomplishes. The doer.*)

The adult adoring the child. The child in adoration of something . . . else. "The Maker?"

"The parent makes the child. The child makes the parent."

"The child *what*?"

Nasive laughed, that full, easy, not "at" kind of laugh which seemed to come so easily to these people. "Come now: whoever became a parent without a child to make him so?"

Charlie laughed with him, but as they left, looked back over his shoulder at the gleaming terra cotta, he knew that Nasive might have said more. And indeed Nasive seemed to understand that, and his feelings about it, for he touched Charlie's elbow and said softly, "Come. I think that later, you will understand better."

Charlie wrenched himself away, but his eyes were full of that exquisite, devout pair shining in the garden. As they crossed the workshop, Charlie asked himself, But why is the child bigger than the parent?

. . . And knew he had asked it aloud when Nasive, stepping into the living room, and incidentally snatching the same youngster they had seen before delightedly cowering in the drapes, and as before scooping it up, turning it over and bumping its little head on the floor until it hiccupped with laughter: "But—children are, you know."

Well . . . in this language, as in English, "bigger" could mean "greater" . . . oh, he'd think about it later. With shining eyes, he looked at the faces in the room, and then felt a very real pang of regret. One ought not to see such a thing, and then have no one new to show it to.

Philos understood, and said, "He's seen your statue. Grocid. Charlie Johns, thank you."

Charlie felt enormously pleased, but, not being able to see his own shining eyes, did not for the life of him know what he was being thanked for.

T HE BRUTE BEGINS OMINOUSLY, STRADDLE-GAITED, HUNCH-shouldered, to approach the bed against which She cowers in her negligee.

"Don't hurt me!" she cries in an Italian accent, whereupon the camera dollies in with the lurch of The Brute, becoming The Brute, and all the blood-and-flesh bugs within the steel-and-chrome beetles ranked up before the gargantuan screen of the drive-in theater, bat their eyes and thrum with the blood in their flesh. The very neon-stained air around the popcorn machines is tumid with it; hooded dead headlights in row upon row seem to bulge with it.

When the camera dollies in close enough to make it possible, for this season cleavage is "in" but the areola is "out," The Brute's big hand darts in from off-camera, smites her ivory cheek stingingly (the straddle-gaited lumbering music stings too) and drops below the frame of the picture, whereupon we hear silk ripping. Her face, still close-up, forty-three tinted feet six inches from tangled hair to dimpled chin, is carried backward by the camera or The Brute and pressed to the satin pillow, whereupon the dark shadow of The Brute's head begins to cover her face with the implacable precision of the studio soundman's hand on a volume knob.

"Don't hurt me! Don't hurt me!"

Herb Raile, behind the wheel of his automobile, is at last made aware of a rhythmic wrestling going on beside him. Although Karen is fast asleep on the back seat, Davy, who at this hour is ordinarily dead to the world, is blaringly wide awake. Jeanette has a half-nelson on the boy and with her other hand is attempting to cover his eyes. Davy is chinning himself on her wrist as on a horizontal bar, and both of them are, in spite of and during this exercise, snatching what avid glances at the screen as they can.

Herb Raile, snatching what avid glances he can at the screen while analyzing this activity, says without turning his head, "What's the *matter*?"

"Nothing for a *child* to see," she hisses. She is a little out of breath from one or another of these stimuli.

"Don't hurt me!" screams shatteringly the She on the screen, then spasms her face and closes her eyes: "Ah-h-h-h-h . . ." she moans, ". . . hurt me. Hurt me. Hurt me. Hurt me."

Davy rips down the blinding hand: "I wanna *see!*"

"You do as you're told or I'll." Herb barks imperatively, watching the screen. Davy sharply nips his mother's forearm. She utters a small scream and says, "Hurt me!"

In not less than seventy feet of super-polychrome three-and-a-quarter-to-one-aspect-ratio tumble-sounded explication, the screen rapidly and succinctly explains that due to an early misunderstanding She and The Brute were actually really and truly married the whole time, and when She has finished, broken in passion and in English as well, explaining to The Brute that the clear source of their excesses is the legality of their loving, the screen dissolves in a blare of light and a blaze of trumpets, leaving the audience limp and blinking in the here and now.

"You shouldn't've let him see all that," says Herb accusingly.

"I didn't but he did. He bit me."

There is an interlude wherein it seems to dawn on Davy that he has done something punishable; he need not know *what* to get it over with, which is done by weeping and being comforted by raspberry sherbet and a shrimp roll. The sherbet, initially on a stick, presents its own problem by leaving same; after a moment of watching it enfold his numb but apparently hot fingertips while it drips exactly on the crease of his trousers, Herb solves the problem by putting it entire into his mouth, which makes the bridge of his nose ache and by which Davy allows he has been robbed. This is not a crisis after all because the lights dim and the screen flares up again for the second feature.

"Something for Davy after all," says Herb after the second minute. "Why don't they run the Western first and spare our kids looking at that kind of you know."

"Sit up on my knee, honey," Jeanette says. "Can you see all right?"

Davy sees all right the fight at the cliff edge, the falling body, the old man lying broken at the foot of the cliff, the evil cowpoke bending over him, the gush of good bright red blood from the old man's mouth: "I'm ... Chuck ... Fritch ... help me!"; the evil cowpoke's laughing, "You're Chuck Fritch are you; that's all I want to know!"; his drawing of the .45, the roaring shots, the twitch of the old man's body as the slugs rip into him and his agonized grunts, the grin on the evil cowboy's face as he stomps the old man's face only they keep that specific off camera, but afterward you can watch him kick the body the rest of the way down into the canyon.

Flashback to a dirt street with duckboard sidewalks. Herb says thoughtfully, "Yeah, I'll call 'em tomorrow, that's what I'll do, ask 'em why they don't put the Westerns on first."

*T*hey went to Wombew's house, the dooryard of which was surrounded by strong and intricate basketwork, which was essentially nothing more than poles driven into the ground and vines woven around them; Wombew, a hawk-nosed young adult, showed Charlie how this was not merely a fence, but was integral with the house, for the walls were built of it too, and then plastered with a clayey mud from the neighborhood—the timeless mud-and-wattle construction—which when quite dry had been coated with a species of whitewash which was not white, but violet. The roof was thatched and planted with the thick-matted, mowing grass found all through Ledom. The house was lovely, especially in its interior planning, for mud-and-wattle need make no compromise with standard lumber lengths, and the more curved the walls, the more stable they are, just as a curved piece of paper may be stood on edge. Grocid and Nasive and their children came along and helped show Charlie Wombew's treasures.

They went to Aborp's house, which had been built of rammed earth, wooden forms having been set up and the moistened earth put between them and compacted by hand with the end of a heavy timber wielded by four strong Ledom standing on the top of the forms. Once it had dried, the forms could be removed. Like the wattle building, this too could be designed very flexibly. Grocid and Nasive and their children and Wombew's children and Wombew came along.

They went to Obtre's house, which was made of cut stone, built up in square modules. Each module had its domed roof, which was made with great simplicity. You fill the four walls right to the top with earth, mound it to suit, and lay on plaster until it is nearly a foot thick. Once it is set, you then dig out all the earth. It is said that this kind of house, with this roof, will stand a thousand years. Obtre and Obtre's children joined them as they went on.

Edec had a moss-chinked log house, Viomor lived right inside a hill, part shored and panelled with hand-rubbed wood, part cut from the living rock. Piante had a fieldstone house with a sod roof, and all the walls were covered with splendid tapestries—not draped, but applied flat so their marvellous pictures and designs could be read; and in the back, Charlie saw the hand-made loom which had made them all, and for a while watched Piante and his mate work the loom, while two tiny children threw the shuttle. And Piante's children and Piante joined them, and his mate, and so did Viomor's family and Edec's; and as they crossed the park areas, people in their bright garments, windblown children and leggy adolescents, came out of the fields and orchards, dropping hoes and mattocks, pruning knives and machetes at the borders, and came along.

As the crowd grew, so grew the music. It was never louder; it grew larger instead.

So at last, visiting and gaining as it went, the multitude, and Charlie Johns, came to the place of worship,

J EANETTE FLINGS HERSELF UNHAPPILY ON THE NEAT AFTERNOON
bed.

What makes me that way?

She has just turned away a home improvement services salesman.
Which is all right in itself. Nobody asks these eager beavers to ring
your doorbell and they have to take their chances. Nobody in her
right mind is going to buy what she doesn't want, and nowadays
you have to get it straight in your head what you don't want and
stick to it, or they'll pull you down, bleed you.

It wasn't that; it was the way she had brushed the man off. She
had acted this way before and doubtless she would again, and that
is what is making her feel so rotten.

Did she have to be that abrupt?

Did she have to give the icy stare, the cold word, the not-quite-
but-very-nearly slammed door? None of that was *her*, was Jeanette.
Could she have done it—get rid of him, that is—acting like Jeanette instead of like some moving-picture parody of the hard life of
a traveling salesman?

Sure she could have.

She sits up. Maybe this time she can think it through and it
won't bother her ever again.

She *has* gotten rid of unwanted sales people, and gotten out of
similar situations, many, many times before by being Jeanette. A
smile, a little lie, something about the baby's waking up or I think

I hear the phone; easy, and no harm done. My husband bought one just day before yesterday. Oh I wish you'd come around last week; I just won one in a contest. Who's to call her a liar? They go away and nobody's hurt.

But then, once in a while, like this one just now, she curls her lip and spits an icicle. And like just now, she stands by the not-quite-slammed door and bites her long coral thumbnail, and then goes to peer unseen through the marquisette curtain, being careful not to move it or touch it, and she watches the way he walks away; she can tell, by the way he walks down the path, that's he's hurt. She's hurt and he's hurt, and who gets anything for it?

She feels rotten.

Why especially him? He wasn't offensive. Far from it. A nice-looking fellow with a good smile, strong teeth, neat clothes, and he wasn't about to shove his foot in the door. He treated her like a lady who might be helped by what he was selling; he was selling that and not himself.

You know, she tells herself, if he had been a real crumb, a winking, eyebrow-waggling creep who'd goggle at the bottom end of your bra strap and make a kissing noise, you'd have told him off in the nice way—a fast, light, harmless brush.

Well, then, she tells herself, appalled, that's the answer. You liked him; that's why you threw the freeze.

She sits on the edge of the bed looking at that idea, and then she closes her eyes and lets her imagination get as foolish as it likes, imagining him coming in, touching her; imagining him right here with her.

And that rings no bell. It really doesn't. What she liked about the man wasn't anything like that at all.

"Now how can you like a man without wanting him?" she demands of herself aloud.

There is no answer. It is an article of faith with her. If you like a man, it has to be because you want him. Whoever heard of it any other way?

People just don't go around liking people on sight unless. And if she can't feel that she wants him, it's one of those subconscious whatcha-ma-callits; she's just not letting herself know it.

She doesn't want to want some other guy besides Herb, but she must. So she's rotten.

She falls back down on the bed and tells herself she ought to be hung up by the thumbs. She's rotten clear through.

*T*he feast was on a mountain—at least, it was the highest hill Charlie had yet seen. Nearly a hundred Ledom were waiting there when Philos and Charlie and the great crowd arrived. In a grove of dark-leaved trees, on the faultless greensward, food was arrayed, laid out Hawaiian fashion on platters of woven fresh leaves and broad grasses. No Japanese flower-arranger ever did a more careful job than these gifted people with their food. Each platter and clever green basket was a construction in color and form, contrast and harmony; and the smells were symphonic.

"Help yourself," smiled Philos.

Charlie looked around him dazedly. The Ledom were coming from every direction, filtering through the trees, greeting each other with glad cries. There were frequent embraces, kisses.

"Where?"

"Anywhere. It's all everybody's."

They stepped through the swirling crowd and seated themselves under a tree. Before them were lovely mounds of food, laid up in graspable, bite-sized portions, and so beautifully arranged that until Philos reached, and disturbed a symmetry, Charlie hadn't the heart to begin.

A pretty child came by with a tray balanced on its head, and a half-dozen mugs apparently designed for the purpose; they were shaped like truncated cones with wide bases. Philos held out a hand and the child skipped toward them; Philos took two mugs and kissed the child, who laughed and danced away. Charlie took a mug and sipped; it was like cool applejuice with peach overtones. He began to eat with enthusiasm. The food tasted as good as it looked—a most extreme statement.

When he was able to slow down enough to look about again, he found the grove thick with a pleasant tension; perhaps it was the cloud of music which hovered over the people that exemplified it most, for it lay in a wide chordal whisper, surging with a pulsation that seemed to become more regular by the moment. One thing that struck Charlie was the fact that a great many people seemed to be feeding each other rather than themselves. He asked about it.

"They're just sharing. If you experience something especially good, don't you feel the need to share it with someone?"

Charlie recalled his odd touch of frustration in the realization that there had been, for him, no one to show the great terra cotta statue to, and said, "I—guess so." He looked at his companion suddenly. "Look—don't let me keep you from uh—joining your friends if you want to."

A strange expression crossed Philos' face. "That is most kind of you," he said warmly. "But I—wouldn't in any case. Not just now." (Was that a slight rush of color in his neck and cheeks? And what was it? Anger? Charlie felt suddenly unwilling to pry.)

"A lot of people," he commented after a while.

"All there are."

"What's the occasion?"

"If you don't mind, I'd like you to tell me what you think, after it's over."

Puzzled, Charlie said, "very well . . ."

They fell silent, listening. Softer and softer became the giant manifold music of the people, humming a series of close, and closely related chords. There crept into it a strange staccato, and looking about him, Charlie saw that some of them were gently tapping themselves, and sometimes their companions, on the base of the throat. It gave the voices a strange thrum, which at last took on a very definite rhythm, rapid but distinct. It seemed an eight-beat, with a slight emphasis on the first and fourth. On this was imposed a low four-tone melody, which cycled, cycled, cycled . . . everyone seemed to crouch, to lean forward a little, to tense . . .

Suddenly came the clarion of a powerful soprano voice, a very cascade of notes, bursting upward like a writhing firework from the drone of the bass melody, and subsiding. It was repeated either from far off in the grove, or from a small voice near by; it was impossible to tell. Two tenors, by some magic striking in a major third apart, repeated the explosion of notes in harmony, and as it faded and fell, another strong voice, a blue-cloaked Ledom seated near Charlie, caught it up and blew it skyward again, this time stripping it of its accidentals and graces and all its *glissandi*, giving it up in its purest form, six clear notes. There was an excited rustle all about, as of appreciation, and a half-dozen scattered voices repeated the six-note theme in unison, then again repeated it. On the second of the six notes, someone else was inspired to start the theme right there; it became fugal, and voice after voice took it up; it burst and fell, burst and fell, interwoven and complex and thrilling. All the while the bass susurrus, with its throat-thumping irregular rhythm, lay under the music, swelling and sighing, swelling greater and drawing back.

Then with a movement as explosive as that first soprano statement, a nude figure came spinning down toward them, weaving in and out between the tree-trunks and among the people; spinning so fast that the body contours were a blur, yet sure-footedly avoiding every obstacle. The spinning Ledom leapt high right by Philos, and came to earth kneeling, face and arms spread on the soft sward. Another came spinning, then another; soon the dark wood was alive with movement, with the swirl of the cloaks and headdresses some wore, with the flash of bodies and blurring limbs. Charlie saw Philos spring to his feet; to his amazement he found himself standing, crouching, buffeted by the rising current of sound and motion. It became an effort not to fling himself into it as into a sea. He drew back finally and clung to the bole of a tree, gasping; for he had an overriding fear that his unschooled feet would never stay under him in the whirling press; that they would be as inadequate to shift and change as were his ears to contain all that was happening in the air about, as were his bewildered eyes to absorb the rush and patterning of those bodies.

It became, for him, a broken series of partial but sharply focussed pictures; the swift turn of a torso; the tense, ecstatic lifting of a fever-blinded head, with the silky hair falling away from the face, and the body trembling; the shrill cry of a little child in transport, running straight through the pattern of the dance, arms outstretched and eyes closed, while the frantic performers, apparently unthinkingly, made way by hairsbreadth after hairsbreadth until a dancer swung about and caught up the infant, *threw* it, and it was plucked out of the air and whirled up again, and once more, to be set down gently at the edge of the dance. At some point unnoted by him, the bass drone had become a roar, and the rhythm, instead of resulting from the subtle tapping of the pharynx, had become a savage beat, furious fists on unnerved thorax and abdomen.

Charlie was shouting. . . .

Philos was gone. . . .

A wave of *something* was generated in the grove, and was released; he could feel it rush him and dissipate; it was as tangible as the radiation from an opened furnace door, but it was not heat. It was not anything he had ever felt, imagined, or experienced before . . . except perhaps by himself . . . oh never by himself; it was with Laura. It was not sex; it was a thing for which sex is one of the expressions. And at this its peak, the harmonious tumult altered in kind, though not at all in quality; the interweaving flesh of the Ledom became a frame circling the children—so many, many children—who had somehow formed themselves into a compact group; they stood proud, even the tiniest ones, proud and knowing and deeply happy, while all about, the Ledom worshipped them, and sang.

They did not sing of the children. They did not sing to the children. It may be said in no other way but this: they sang the children.

SMITTY HAS COME OUT TO CHAT OVER THE BACK FENCE—ACTUALLY, it is a low stone wall—with Herb. It happens that Smitty is sick furious with Tillie over something that does not matter really. Herb has been sitting on a lawn chair under a red and white umbrella with the afternoon paper, and he is furious also, but with somewhat less sickness and impersonally as well. Congress has not only passed a particularly stupid bill, but has underscored its particular stupidity by overriding a presidential veto. Seeing Smitty, he throws down the paper and strides to the back wall.

"How come," he says, meaning it purely as a preliminary remark, "the world is so full of dirty sons of bitches?"

"That's easy," is the instant, dour remark. "Every one of 'em was born out of the dirtiest part of a woman."

*T*hough in Ledom it never grew dark, it seemed darker with most of the people gone. Charlie sat on the cool green moss with his wrists on his kneecaps and his back against an olive tree, and bent his head to put his cheeks against the backs of his hands. His cheeks felt leathery, for there unaccountable tears had dried. At length he straightened up and looked at Philos, who waited patiently beside him.

Philos, as though to be sure not to utter a word lest it spoil something for his guest, acknowledged him with a soft smile and a peaking of his odd eyebrows.

"Is it over?" Charlie asked.

Philos leaned back against the tree, and with a motion of his head indicated a group of Ledom, three adults and a half-dozen children, far down the grove, who were cheerfully picking up the mess. Over them, like an invisible swarm of magic bees, hung a cloud of music, at that moment triads, minor thirds, winging neatly upwards in formation, hovering, fading winging upwards again. "It's never over," Philos said.

Charlie thought about that, and the statue called *The Maker*, and about as much as he dared to think about what had passed in the grove, and about the sound which dwelt about these people wherever they gathered.

Philos asked, quietly, "Do you want to ask me again what this place is?"

Charlie shook his head and got to his feet. "I think I know," he said.

"Come, then," said Philos.

They walked to the fields, and through and by the fields and cottages, back toward the Ones, and they talked:

"Why do you worship children?"

Philos laughed. It was pleasure, mostly. "First of all, I suppose it's because religion—and just to preclude argument, I'll define religion for this purpose as the supra-rational, or mystic experience—it's because religion seems to be a necessity to the species—but it would seem as well that the experience is not possible without an object. There is nothing more tragic than a person or a culture who, feeling the need to worship, has no object for it."

"For the sake of no argument, as you say, I'll buy that" said Charlie, aware of how quaint that sounded in Ledom. The word for "buy" was "interpenetrate"—a derivation of "exchange"—but surprisingly, shy as he might from its overtones in the place, his meaning emerged. "But why children?"

"We worship the future, not the past. We worship what is to come, not what has been. We aspire to the consequences of our own acts. We keep before us the image of that which is malleable and growing—of that which we have the power to improve. We worship that very power in ourselves, and the sense of responsibility which lives with it. A child is all of these things. Also . . ." and he stopped.

"Go on."

"It's something which you need a good deal of adjustment to absorb, Charlie. I don't think you can do it."

"Try me."

Philos shrugged. "You asked for it: We worship the child because it is inconceivable that we would ever obey one."

They walked in silence for a long time.

"What's the matter with obeying the God you worship?"

"In theory, nothing, I suppose, especially when along with the obedience goes the belief in a living—that is, current, and contemporaneously knowledgeable God." Philos paused, choosing words.

"But in practice, more often than not, the hand of God in human affairs is a dead hand. His dictates are couched in the interpretations of Elders of one kind and another—past-drenched folk with their memories impaired, their eyes blinded, and all the love in them dried up." He looked at Charlie, and his dark strange eyes were full of compassion. "Haven't you been able to see yet that the very essence of the Ledom is—passage?"

"Passage?"

"Movement, growth, change, catabolism. Could music exist without passage, without progression, or poetry; could you speak a word and call it a rhyme without speaking more words? Could life exist . . . why, passage is very nearly a definition for life! A living thing changes by the moment and by each portion of each part of a moment; even when it sickens, even when it decays, it changes, and when it stops changing, it's—oh, it could be many things; lumber, like a dead tree; food, like a killed fruit; but it's not life anymore. . . . The architecture of a culture is supposed to express its state of mind, if not its very faith; what do the shapes of the Medical One and the Science One say to you?"

Charlie snickered; it was the laugh of unease, like embarrassment. *"Tim . . . ber!"* he cried in an imitation bellow, in English. Then he explained, "That's what the loggers used to shout when they'd cut through a tree-trunk and it was about to fall: get out of the way!"

Philos laughed appreciatively and without rancor. "Have you ever seen a picture of a man running? Or even walking? He is off balance, or would be if he were as frozen as the picture is. He could hardly run or walk if he weren't imbalanced. That is how you progress from any place to any other place—by beginning, over and over again, to fall."

"And then it turns out they're propped up on invisible crutches."

Philos twinkled, "All symbols are, Charlie."

Again, Charlie was forced to laugh. " 'There's only one Philos.' " He said it with unconscious mimicry. And again, he saw Philos flush darkly. Anger—for that matter, even mild irritation—was so rare here that it was more shocking than profanity. "What's the matter? Did I—"

"Who said that? Mielwis, wasn't it?" Philos shot him a sharp glance, and read the answer from Charlie's face. He apparently read also the necessity for the end of anger, for with an obvious effort he put his down, and pleaded: "Don't feel you've said anything wrong, Charlie. It isn't you at all. Mielwis . . ." He drew and released a deep breath. "Mielwis occasionally indulges in a private joke." Abruptly and, with evident purpose, changing the subject, he demanded, "But about the architecture—don't you quarrel with the concept of dynamic imbalance in the face of these?" He swept his hand to indicate the cottages—mud-and-wattle, rammed earth, log and plaster and stone and hewn planks.

"Nothing tottery about that," agreed Charlie, nodding toward the one they were passing—the Italian square-module one with the domed plaster roofs over each square.

"So they're not symbols. Or not in the sense that the big Ones are. They're the concrete results of our profound conviction that the Ledom will never separate themselves from the land—and I mean that in its widest possible sense. Civilizations have a pernicious way of breeding whole classes and generations of people who make their livings once removed—twice, ten, fifty times removed from the techniques of the hand. Men could be born, live, and die, and never move a spade of earth, or true a timber, or weave a swatch, or even see spade, adze or loom. Isn't that so, Charlie? Wasn't it so with you?"

Charlie nodded thoughtfully. He had had the same thought himself—he really had, one day when, city-bred as he was, he hired out to pick beans once when he needed the money and there was an ad in the paper. He had hated it, living in barracks with a filthy herd of human misfits, and working all day in cramping, crouching, baking, soaking labor for which he was untrained and in which—even the matter of picking beans—he was unskilled. Yet it had come to him that just this once, when once he actually ate a bean, that he himself was taking from the womb of the soil that which it bore and which could in turn sustain him. He was putting his two naked hands to the naked earth, and between him and it was no complex of interchange, status, substitution, or intricate many-layered system of barter between goods and services. And it had come to him again more than once since, when the intimate, earthy matter of filling his belly was taken care of by making marks on paper, by scraping and stacking restaurant plates and scrubbing pots, by pulling steering clutches on a bulldozer or pushing buttons on an adding machine.

"Such men have an extremely limited survival value," Philos was saying. "They have, like good survival creatures, adapted to their environment—but that environment is a large and elaborate machine; there is very little about it which is as basic as the simple act of plucking a fruit or finding and cooking the proper grass. Should the machine be smashed, or should even some small but integral part of it stop working, everyone in it will become a hopeless dependent in precisely the length of time it takes his stomach to empty itself. *All* the Ledom—every single one of us—though we might find ourselves with one or two real skills, have a working knowledge of agriculture and basic construction, weaving, cooking, and waste disposal, and how to make fire and find water. Skilled or no—and no one is skilled in everything—an unskilled person with a working knowledge of necessities is better able to survive than a man who could, say, control a sheet-metal mill better than anyone else in the world but does not know how to join a rafter or save seedcorn or dig a latrine."

"Oh-h-h," said Charlie in tones of revelation.

"What is it?"

"I'm beginning to see something here . . . I couldn't square all that push-button living in the Medical One with all the hand-made crockery. I thought it was a matter of privilege."

"Those who work in the Ones eat out here as a privilege!" (Actually, the word "privilege" here is not exact; it translated "favor" or "treat.") "The Ones are first of all working places, and the only places where the work from time to time is so exacting and must be done with such precision that it is efficient to save time. Out here it is efficient to use time; we have so much of it. We do not sleep, and no matter how carefully you build or cultivate, the work keeps getting finished."

"How much time do the children spend in school?"

"School—oh. Oh, I see what you mean. No, we don't have schools."

"No schools? But . . . oh, that is good enough for people who only want to know how to plant and build do-it-yourself housing . . . is that what you mean? But—what about your technologists— you don't live forever, do you? What happens when one needs replacing? And what about books . . . and music manuscript . . . and—oh, all the things that people learn to read and write for? Mathematics—reference books—"

"We don't need them. We have the cerebrostyle."

"Seace mentioned it. I can't say I understand it."

"I can't say that either," said Philos. "But I can assure you it works."

"And you use it for teaching, instead of schools."

"No. Yes."

Charlie laughed at him.

Philos laughed too, and said, "I wasn't as confused as I sounded. The 'no' was for your statement, we use the cerebrostyle for teaching. We don't *teach* our children the 'book' kind of learning, we implant it with the cerebrostyle. It's quick—it's only a matter of selecting the right information block and throwing a switch. The (he here used a technical term for "unused and available memory cells") and the synaptic paths to them are located and the information 'printed' on the mind in a matter of seconds—one and a half, I think. Then the block is ready for the next person. But *teaching*, now; well, if there is any teaching done with this implanted information, you do it yourself, either by consciously thinking it through—much faster than reading by the way—while you're work-ing in the fields, or during a 'pause'—remember the Ledom we saw standing alone just before we got to Grocid's house? . . . But even that process you can't call teaching. Teaching is an art that can be learned; learning from a teacher is an art that can be learned; anyone who tries—and we all try—can gain a certain competence in teaching; but a *real* teacher, now—he has a talent. He has a gift like a fine artist or musician or sculptor. Oh, we think highly of teachers, and of teaching. Teaching is part of loving, you know," he added.

Charlie thought of cold, repellent, dying Miss Moran and understood in a great warm flash. He thought of Laura.

"We use the cerebrostyle," said Philos, "as we use the A-field; we don't depend on it. We don't, therefore, *need* it. We learn reading and writing, and we have a great many books; any Ledom who cares to may read them, although we generally like to have him put on the cerebrostyle 'setter' while he reads, and make a new block."

"These blocks—they can hold a whole book?"

Philos held up two thumbnails, side by side. "In about that much space. . . . And we know how to make paper and manufacture books, and if we ever had to, we would. You must understand that about us; we shall never, never be the slaves of our conveniences."

"That's good," said Charlie, thinking of many, many past things which were not good; thinking of whole industries crippled when the elevator operators went on strike in a central office building, thinking of the plight of a city apartment dweller during a power failure, without water, refrigeration, lights, radio, television; unable to cook, wash, or be amused. But . . . "Even so," he mused, "There's something about it I don't like. If you can do that you can select a block and implant a whole set of beliefs and loyalties; you could arrange a slavery that would make any of ours look like a practice hop in a sack race."

"No we *can't!*" Philos said forcefully. "To say nothing of the fact that we wouldn't. You don't love, nor gain love, by imprisonment or command, or by treachery and lies."

"You don't?" asked Charlie.

"The parts of the mind are now clearly defined. The cerebrostyle is an information transfer device. The only way you could implant false doctrines would be to simultaneously shut off all other memory plus all the senses; because I assure you that whatever the cerebrostyle gives you is subject to review against everything you already know plus everything you experience. We could not reach inconsistencies if we tried."

"Do you ever withhold information?"

Philos chuckled. "You do hunt for flaws, now, don't you?"

"Well," said Charlie, "do you ever withhold information?"

The chuckle clicked off. Philos said soberly, "Of course we do. We wouldn't tell a child how to prepare fuming nitric acid. We wouldn't tell a Ledom how his mate screamed under a rock-fall."

"Oh." They walked a while in silence. . . . a Ledom and his mate . . . "You do marry, then?"

"Oh yes. To be lovers is a happy thing. But to be married—that is happiness on a totally different level. It is a solemn thing among us, and we take it very seriously. You know Grocid and Nasive."

A light dawned in Charlie's mind. "They dress alike."

"They do everything alike, or if not alike, then together. Yes, they're married."

"Do you . . . do the people . . . uh . . ."

Philos clapped him on the shoulder. "I know about your preoccupation in the matter of sex," he said. "Go on—ask me. You're among friends."

"I'm *not* preoccupied with it!"

They walked on, Charlie sullenly, Philos humming softly, suddenly, in harmony with a distant melody that drifted down to them from some children in the fields. Hearing it, Charlie's sullenness abruptly lifted. He realized that these things are, after all, comparative; the Ledom genuinely were less preoccupied with sexual matters than he was, just as he was less preoccupied than, say, a Victorian housewife who would refer to the "limbs" of a piano, and who would not put a book by a male author on a shelf next to one by a female author unless the two authors happened to be married.

And he was prepared to accept, as well, Philos' statement that he was among friends.

As conversationally as possible, he asked, "What about children?"

"What about children?"

"Suppose one—ah—gets born and the—ah—parent isn't married?"

"Most of them are born that way."

"And it makes no difference?"

"Not to the child. Not to the parent, either, as far as anyone else is concerned."

"Then what's the point of getting married?"

"The point, Charlie, is that the whole is greater than the sum of its parts."

"Oh."

"The greatest occasion of sexual expression is a mutual orgasm, wouldn't you say?"

"Yes," said Charlie as clinically as he could.

"And procreation is a high expression of love?"

"Oh yes."

"Then if a Ledom and his mate mutually conceive, and each bears twins, does not that appear to be a fairly transcendant experience?"

"F-fairly," said Charlie in a faint voice, overwhelmed. He put the transcendence away in the back of his mind, kneeing it down until it stopped making quite so large a lump. When he could, he asked, "What about the other kind of sex?"

"*Other* kind?" Philos wrinkled his brow, and apparently went through some sort of mental card-file. "Oh—you mean just ordinary expressive sex."

"I suppose that's what I mean."

"Well, it happens, that's all. Anything which is an expression of love can happen here, sex, or helping put on a roof, or singing." Glancing at Charlie's face, he nodded to his invisible card-file and went on: "I think I know what's perplexing you. You come from a place where certain acts and expressions were held in a bad light—frowned upon, even punished. Is that it?"

"I guess."

"Then apparently this is what you want to know: There is no opprobrium connnected with it here. It isn't regulated in any way. It can only happen when it's an expression of mutual affection, and if there isn't mutual affection, it doesn't happen."

"What about the young"

"What *about* the young?"

"I mean . . . kids, you know. Experimenting and all that."

Philos laughed his easy laugh. "Question: When are they old enough to do it? Answer: When they are old enough to do it. As for experimentation, why experiment with anything that's almost as commonly seen as the greeting kiss?"

Charlie gulped. Put this where he may, it still made a lump. Almost plaintively, he said, "But—what about unwanted children?"

Philos stopped dead, turned, and looked at him, his dark face showing an almost comic succession of changes: shock, amazement, disbelief, question (Are you kidding? Do you mean what you just said?); and at length, of all things, apology. "I'm sorry, Charlie, I didn't think you could shock me, but you did. I thought that after the amount of research I've done, I was proof against it, but I guess I never expected to stand here in the middle of Ledom and try to engage my mind with the concept of an *unwanted* child."

"I'm sorry, Philos. I didn't mean to shock anybody."

"*I'm* sorry. I am surprised that I was shocked, and sorry that I showed it."

Then, through an orchard, Grocid hailed them, and Philos asked, "You thirsty?" and they struck off toward the white cottage. It was good, for a while, to be able to get their attention away from one another. It was good to be able to go out and look at the terra cotta again.

Herb stands in the moonstruck dark looking down at his daughter. He has slipped out of bed and come here because, on other occasions, he has found it a good place to be for the distraught, the confused, the hurt and puzzled mind. It is not easy to contain feelings of violence and unrest while, breathless, one leans close to examine by moonlight the meeting of the eyelids of a sleeping child.

His malaise began three days ago, when his neighbor Smith, in bitter casualness, tossed a remark over the back wall. The statement itself had seemed, at the time, to go by him like a bad odor; he had chatted about a political matter and the talk had then dwindled away to inconsequence. Yet since then he found he had taken the remark away with him; it was as if Smitty, having been plagued by some festering growth, had been able to drive it into his, Herb's flesh.

It is with him now and he cannot put it by.

Men are born out of the dirtiest part of a woman.

Herb dissociates the remark from Smith, a man who has his troubles and his especial background, for neither of which he is completely accountable. What is troubling Herb Raile is an issue far larger; he is wondering what it is about humanity, since it first came out of the trees, in all that many different things it has been and done, which makes it possible for even one man to say once a thing as filthy as that.

Or was it more than an obscene joke . . . is it true, or nearly true?

Is that what is meant by the inescapable taint of Original Sin? Is it men's disgust of women that makes so many of them treat women with such contempt? Is it that which makes it so easy to point out that the Don Juans and the Lotharios, for all their hunger for women, are often merely trying to see how many women they can punish? Is this the realization which makes a man, having like a good Freudian child passed into a period of mother-fixation, find a turning point and begin to hate his mother?

When did men begin to find womanhood despicable—when did they decree the menses unclean, and even to this day practice in their houses of worship the ritual known as "churching of women" —the old post-natal purification ceremony?

Because I don't feel that way, he says silently and devoutly. I love Jeanette because she is a woman, and I love her all over.

Happily, Karen sighs in her sleep. The anger and terror and outrage of his thoughts tumble away, and he smiles over Karen, yearns over her.

Nobody, he thinks, ever wrote anything about father-love. Mother-love is supposed to be a magic expression of the hand of God or something, or maybe the activity of certain ductless glands; it depends on who's talking. But father-love . . . an awful funny thing, father-love. He's seen an otherwise mild and civilized man go clean berserk because "somebody did something to my kid." He knows from his own experience that after a while this father-love thing begins to spread out; you begin to feel that way, a little, toward all kids. Now where's that come from? The kid never inhabits the abdomen, doesn't pull on and feed off the body, as with women; mother love makes sense, it figures; a baby grows on and of the mother's flesh like a nose. But the father? Why, it takes some pretty special circumstances to make a father even remember the particular two-or three-second spasm that did the job.

Why wouldn't it ever occur to anyone to say humanity was full of sons of bitches because it issued from the filthiest part of a man? It wouldn't, you know; not ever.

Because, it says here, man is superior. Man—mankind (and oh yes, women have learned this trick!), mankind has in it a crushing need to feel superior. This doesn't have to bother the very small minority who actually are superior, but it sure troubles the controlling majority who are not. If you can't be really good at anything, then the only way to be able to prove you are superior is to make someone else inferior. It is this rampaging need in humanity which has, since pre-history, driven a man to stand on the neck of his neighbor, a nation to enslave another, a race to tread on a race. But it is also what men have always done to women.

Did they actually find them inferior to begin with, and learn from that to try to feel superior to other things outside—other races, religions, nationalities, occupations?

Or was it the other way around: did men make women inferior for the same reason they tried to dominate the outsider? Which is cause, which effect?

And—isn't it just self-preservation? Wouldn't women dominate men if they had the chance?

Aren't they trying it right now?

Haven't they already done it, here on Begonia Drive?

He looks down at Karen's hand in the moonlight. He saw it first when it was an hour old, and was thunderstruck by the perfection of the fingernails, of all things; so tiny! so tiny! so perfect! And is this little hand to take hold of reins, Karen, or pull strings. Karen? Are you come into a world where down deep the world despises you, Karen?

The father-love suffuses him, and unmoving, yet he sees in a transported moment himself standing like a warrior between the slime-born sons of bitches and his child.

*"N*asive ..."

The Ledom, glowing with preasure, stood before the terra cotta group with Charlie, smiled and answered, "Yes?"

"Can I ask you something?"

"Anything."

"Confidential, Nasive. Is it wrong to ask you that?"

"I don't think so."

"And if I step out of bounds in asking, you won't take it poorly? I'm a stranger here."

"Ask me."

"It's about Philos."

"Oh."

"Why is everyone here so hard on Philos? Let me take that back," he amended quickly. "That puts it too strongly. It's just that everyone seems to sort of ... disapprove. Not so much of him, but of something about him."

"Oh," said Nasive, "I don't think it's anything that matters very much."

"You're not going to tell me, then." There was a stiff silence. Then Charlie said, "I'm supposed to be learning all I can about Ledom. Do you or do you not think I would gain some kind of insight by knowing something that was wrong in Ledom? Or am I supposed to judge you only by—" he nodded at the statue—"what you like best about yourselves?"

As he had seen Philos do before, Charlie watched a Ledom instantly and completely disarmed. The impact of truth on these folk was, apparently, enormous.

"You couldn't be more right, Charlie Johns, and I shouldn't have hesitated. But—in all fairness to Philos. I must in turn ask *your* confidence. The matter is, after all, Philos' business and not mine nor yours."

"I won't let him know I know."

"Very well, then. Philos stands a little apart from the rest of us. For one thing, he has a secretiveness about him—which in a way is useful; he is given access to a great many things which the rest of us are better off without. But one feels that he . . . prefers it that way, while to the normal Ledom, that sort of thing might be a duty, but it would be an onerous one.

"That doesn't seem reason enough to—"

"Oh, it isn't the prime discomfort he generates! The other thing about him—perhaps it is part of the same thing—is that he won't marry."

"A person doesn't *have* to marry, does he?"

"Oh no indeed." Nasive moistened his full lips and frowned. "But Philos behaves as if he is still married."

"*Still* married?"

"He was married to Froure. They were to have children. One day they walked out to the edge of the sky—" (Charlie comprehended the odd phrase)—"and there was an accident. A rock-slide. They were buried for days. Froure was killed. Philos lost the unborn children."

Charlie recalled that Philos had used "screaming in a rock-slide" as a figure of speech.

"Philos grieved . . . well, we can all understand that. We love a great deal, we love many ways; our mates we love deeply indeed, and so we understand the nature of grief. But as basic with us as love itself is the necessity to love the living, not the dead. It makes us feel . . . uncomfortable . . . to have someone around who holds himself aloof from loving freely, to be faithful to someone who is gone. It's . . . pathological."

"Maybe he'll get over it."

"It happened many years ago," said Nasive, shaking his head.

"If it's pathological, can't you treat it?"

"With his agreement, we could. And since his particular quirk presents nothing worse than a mild discomfort for a few of us, he is free to remain the way he is if that's what he wishes."

"Now I understand that little joke of Mielwis."

"What was that?"

"He said, 'There's only one like him!' but he said it as a joke."

"That was hardly worthy of Mielwis," said Nasive sternly.

"Whatever it was, it's confidential."

"Of course. . . . And now do you feel you know us any better?"

"I don't," said Charlie, "but I feel I will."

They exchanged smiles and returned to the house to join the others. Philos was deep in conversation with Grocid, and Charlie was certain they were talking about him. Grocid confirmed this by saying, "Philos tells me you're almost ready to pass judgment on us."

"Not exactly that," laughed Philos. "It's just that I've given you almost all I have. How long it takes you to draw your conclusions is up to you."

"I hope it's a long time," said Grocid. "You're very welcome here, you know. Nasive likes you."

It was the kind of remark which in Charlie's day might be made out of the subject's presence, but not in it. Charlie glanced swiftly at Nasive, only to find him nodding. "Yes, I do," said Nasive warmly.

"Well, thanks," said Charlie. "I like it here too."

"SMITH IS A SWINE."

Herb Raile, preoccupied, hears these words from Jeanette as she comes in the back door after a visit with Tillie, and he starts violently. He has shared none of his recent thoughts about Smith with her nor with anyone, though he feels a great need to unburden himself. He had checked over all possible recipients for his pressures—one of the girls, maybe, who hung around after the League of Women Voters meetings, or some of the folks at the Great Books gatherings, or the P.T.A., although as the father of a five-year-old he was only peripherally involved there as yet, likewise the local School Board Association. But he is afraid. Swine or no, Smith's advice was sound: A new account—that's serious. Anything else, kicks.

He is not getting any kicks at all out of this thing; it's too large for him and it is not crystallized. Surprised as he is over the confluence of Jeanette's remark to his thoughts, he is not even sure yet whether he thinks Smith is a swine. A pig among people is a pig, he tells himself, but a pig among pigs is people.

"What's he done?"

"You go over there, that's all. He'll show it to you. Tillie's just wild."

"I wish I knew what you are talking about, honey."

"I'm sorry, honey. It's a sign thing, a sort of plaque in the rumpus room."

"Something like those urinary-type labels for the liquor bottles?"

"Much worse. You'll see."

"**W**hat's next, Philos?"

"A good hard look at yourself," said Philos, and then turned and took the edge off the words with a warm smile. "A categorical 'yourself,' I mean. You wouldn't want to evaluate Ledom in a vacuum. Much better to be able to set it up against the other culture for contrast."

"I already can, I think. In the first place—" but Philos was interrupting:

"You can?" he said, with such meaning that Charlie shut up.

They were walking the final mile between the Children's One and the Science One. A little petulantly, Charlie said, "I know enough about my own people, I think, to—"

Again Philos sardonically interrupted, and said, "You do?"

"Well, if you don't think so," said Charlie with some heat, "go ahead!"

"Go ahead and what?"

"Set me straight."

"I am," said Philos, taking no offense and, strangely, giving none. "We're going to do it with the cerebrostyle. Quicker, easier, much more detailed, and," he grinned, "inarguable and uninterruptible."

"I wouldn't interrupt and argue."

"You would; you must. There is literally no subject ever encountered in the history of mankind so unsusceptible to objective study as that of sex. Countless volumes have been written about history and historical motivations with never a mention of sex. Entire generations, and scores of successive generations, of students have pored over them and taken them for the truth and the whole truth, and some have gone on to teach the same things in the same way—even when the importance of sex motivations to the individual had been revealed, even when the individual, in his daily life, was interpreting his whole world with them, filling his thoughts and his language with sex referents. Somehow history remained to a great majority of people a series of anecdotes about some strangers who performed acts and fulfilled desires strangely separated from the sexual behavior of their times—behavior which was at once the result and the cause of their acts. Behavior which produced both history and the blind historian . . . and, I suppose, his blindness as well. But I should be saying these things after you're through the course, and not before."

"I think," said Charlie a little stiffly, "we'd better get to it."

They walked round the Science One and took the subway to the Medical One, and Philos led Charlie through the now-familiar horizontal catacombs and vertiginous flights of the huge building. Once they passed through a good-sized hall, rather like a railroad waiting room; it was full of the Ledom chordal hum and the soft cooing of their voices; Charlie was particularly struck by the tableau of two identically cloaked Ledom, each with a sleeping child on the knees, each nursing another . . . "What are they all waiting for?"

"I think I told you—everyone comes here each twenty-eight days for a checkup."

"Why?"

"Why not? Ledom is small, you know—we haven't eight hundred people yet—and no one lives more than two hours' walk away. We have all the facilities, so—why not?"

"How thorough is the checkup?"

"*Very.*"

Near the top of the building Philos stopped in front of a doorslit. "Palm it—there."

Charlie did so, and nothing happened. Then Philos palmed it and it opened. "My private preserve," said Philos. "The nearest thing to a lock you will find in all Ledom."

"Why lock anything?" Charlie had noticed the absence of locks, especially throughout the Children's One.

Philos waved Charlie in, and the door snapped shut. "We have very few taboos in Ledom," he said, "but one of them is against leaving highly contagious material around." He was half-joking, Charlie knew; yet there was a strong serious element in what he said. "Actually," Philos explained, "few Ledom would bother with this," and he waved a hand carelessly at a half-dozen floor-to-ceiling bookshelves and a wall-rack of small stacked transparent cubes. "We're infinitely more concerned with the future, and none of this matters much any more. Still . . . 'man, know thyself' . . . It might make some folks pretty unhappy to know themselves this well."

He went to the rack of cubes, consulted an index, and took down a cube. In purple, it bore a small line of numbers; he checked this against the index and then went to a low couch and, from one of the magically-appearing wall niches, drew a piece of apparatus. It was a bowl-shaped helmet supported by a jointed arm. "The cerebrostyle," he said. He tipped it up so Charlie could look inside the bowl. It showed nothing but a dozen or so rubbery nubbins, set into its crown. "No electrodes, no probes. And it doesn't hurt a bit."

He took his small numbered cube, opened a chamber near the top of the helmet, dropped the cube in, closed and clamped the lid. Then he lay on the couch, drew the helmet down and pressed it against his head. The instrument seemed to tilt a bit, forward and back, finding purchase, orienting.

It ceased to move, and Philos relaxed. He smiled up at Charlie, and said, "Now excuse me a couple of seconds." He closed his eyes, reached up and touched a stud at the edge of the helmet. The stud remained depressed; his hand fell limply away.

There was a deep silence.

The stud clicked, and instantly Philos opened his eyes. He

pushed away the helmet and sat up. There was no sign of fatigue or strain. "That didn't take long, did it?"

"What did you do?"

Philos pointed to the little hatchway into which he had dropped the cube. "That's a little dissertation I prepared on certain aspects of homo sap.," he said. "It needed a little . . . editing. There are certain facts you say you do not wish to know, and besides, I wanted it to come to you from me, like a letter, rather than impersonally, like a textbook."

"You mean you can alter these records, just like that?"

"It takes a little practice, and a deal of concentration, but—yes. Well—go ahead." When Charlie looked at the helmet and hesitated, Philos laughed at him. "Go on. It won't hurt, and it'll bring you that much closer to home."

Boldly, then, Charlie Johns lay down. Philos swung the helmet over him and helped him place it over his head. Charlie felt the blunt little fingers inside touch his scalp, cling. The helmet moved, and then was still. Philos took his hand and guided it to the stud. "Push this yourself, when you're ready. Nothing will happen until you do." He stepped back. "Relax."

Charlie looked up at him. There was no spite or slyness in the strange dark eyes; only warm encouragement.

He pressed the stud.

Herb crosses the back yard, wondering how to ask Smitty about the plaque, or whatever it was, that had steamed Jeanette up so, without actually informing him that Jeanette is angry.

Smitty is poking at a border of marigolds, and when he sees Herb, he gets up, dusts off his knees, and solves the problem:

"Hi. Come on over; I want to show you something. Think you'll get a charge out of it."

Herb vaults the low wall and goes with Smith into the house and down the steps. Smith has a nice rumpus room. The heater looks like a hi-fi-set and the hi-fi set looks like a radiator. The washer-dryer looks like a television, the television looks like a coffee table, the bar looks like a bar, and the whole business is in knotty pine.

Over the bar in front-and-center position, well framed and glazed, in large gothic or black-letter script, so you have to read it slowly and it's all the funnier for that, is a quotation which declares itself (down at the end in fine print) vaguely as the work of "a Middle Ages Philosopher":

> A Good Woman (as an old Philosopher observeth) is like one Ele put in a bagge amongst 500 Snakes, and if a man should have the luck to grope out that one Ele from all the Snakes, yet he hath at best but a wet Ele by the Taile.

Herb is prepared to join Jeanette in indignation, sight unseen, but the plaque takes him deliciously by surprise, and he roars, while Smitty chuckles in the background. Then Herb asks how Tillie likes it.

"Women," Smitty pontificates, "are squares."

*P*hilos had said it well: it was like a letter. "Reading" it, however, was unlike anything he had ever experienced consciously before. He had pressed the stud, which emitted a soft *chuck!*, and then there was a passage of time which was measureless, in that the mental clock which tells a man, unthinking, whether a bell rang five seconds, five minutes, or five hours ago, was momentarily stopped or suspended. It could not have been very long, however, and there was, in any ordinary sense, no loss of awareness, for when the stud went *chuck!* again, Philos still stood over him, smiling. But he now felt precisely as if, at that very moment, he had put down, after an absorbed reading, a long and interesting letter from a friend.

He said, startled into English, "Well, for *God's* sake!"

Charlie Johns, [the "letter" had begun] you cannot be objective about this discussion. But try. Please try.

You cannot be objective about it because you have been indoctrinated, sermonized, drenched, imbued, inculcated and policed on the matter since first you wore blue booties. You come from a time and place in which the maleness of the male, and the femaleness of the female, and the importance of their difference, were matters of almost total preoccupation.

Begin, then, with this—and if you like, regard it as mainly a working hypothesis. Actually it is a truth, and if at the end it passes the tests of your own understanding, you will see that it is a truth. If you do not, the fault is not with you, but with your orientation:

There are more basic similarities than differences between men and women.

Read through an anatomy manual. A lung is a lung, a kidney a kidney in man or in woman. It may be that statistically, women's bone-structure was lighter, the head smaller, and so on and on; yet it is not impossible that mankind had, for many thousands of years, bred for that. But aside from such conjectures, the variations permissible to what is called "normal" structure provide many examples of women who were taller, stronger, heavier-boned than most men, and men who were smaller, slighter, lighter than most women. Many men had larger pelvic openings than many women.

In the area of the secondary sexual characteristics, it is only statistically that we can note signifcant differences; for many women had more body hair than many men; many men had higher-pitched voices than many women. . . . I call again on your objectivity: suspend for a moment your conviction that the statistical majority is the norm, and examine the cases, in their vast numbers, which exist outside that probable fiction, that norm. And go on:

For even with the sex organs themselves, variations in development—and here, admittedly, we approach the pathological—have yielded countless cases of atrophied phalli, hypertrophied clitori, perforate rathes, detached labia . . . all, viewed *objectively,* reasonably subtle variations from the norm, and capable of producing, on an initially male or female body, virtually identical urogenital triangles. It is not my intention to state that such a situation is or should be normal—at least not after the fourth fetal month, though up to then it is not only normal but universal—but only to bring out to you that its occurrence is easily within the limits of what has been, since prehistory, possible to nature.

Endocrinology demonstrates a number of interesting facts. Both male and female could produce male and female hormones, and did, and as a matter of fact, the preponderance of one over the other was a subtle matter indeed. Then if you throw that delicate balance out, the changes which could be brought about were drastic. In a few months you could produce a bearded and breastless lady and a man whose nipples, no longer an atrophied insigne of the very point I am making here, could be made to lactate.

These are gross and extreme examples purely for illustration. There have been many women athletes who could exceed in strength, speed and skill the vast majority of men, but who were nonetheless what you might call "real" women, and many men who could, say, design clothing—traditionally a woman's specialty—far better than most women, yet who were what you might call "real" men. For when we get into what I might broadly term cultural differences between the sexes, the subtlety of sexual distinction begins to become apparent. What say the books:

Women have long hair. So have the Sikhs, whom some call the toughest breed of soldiers ever bred. So had the 18th-century cavaliers, and brocaded jackets and lace at throat and wrists as well. Women wear skirts. So does a kilted Scot, a Greek *evzone*, a Chinese, a Polynesian, none of whom could deserve the term "effeminate."

An objective scan of human history proliferates these examples to numbers astronomical. From place to place, and in any place from time to time, the so-called "provinces" of male and female rise like the salinity of a tidal river-mouth, mingling, separating, ebbing and regrouping . . . before your first World War, cigarettes and wrist-watches were regarded as unquestionably female appurtenances; twenty years later both were wholeheartedly adopted by the men. Europeans, especially central Europeans, were startled and very much amused to see American farmers milking cows and feeding chickens, for never in their lives had they seen that done by any but women.

So it is easily seen that the sexual insignes are nothing in themselves, for any of them, in another time and place, might belong to both sexes, the other sex, or neither. In other words, a skirt does not make the social entity, woman. It takes a skirt plus a social attitude to do it.

But all through history, in virtually every culture and country, there has indeed been a "woman's province" and a "man's province," and in most cases the differences between them have been exploited to fantastic, sometimes sickening extremes.

Why?

First of all, it is easy to state, and easy to dispose of, the theory that in a primitive, primarily hunting-and-fishing society, a weaker, slower-moving sex, occasionally heavy with child and forced frequently to pause to nurse her young, is not as well fitted to hunt and fight as the fleeter-footed, untrammeled, hard-muscled male. However, it may well be that the primitive woman was not that much smaller, slower, weaker than her mate. Perhaps the theory confuses cause and effect, and perhaps, if some other force had not insisted upon such a development, accepted it, even bred for it, the nonparous females might have hunted with the best of the men, while those men who happened to be slower, smaller, weaker, kept house with the pregnant and nursing women. And this has happened—not in the majority of cases, but many times nevertheless.

The difference existed—granted. But it was exploited. It was a difference which continued to exist long, long after there was any question of hunting or, for that matter, of nursing. Humanity has insisted upon it; made it an article of faith. Again:

Why?

It would seem that there *is* a force which widens and exploits this difference, and, isolated, it is a deplorable, even terrifying pressure.

For there is in mankind a deep and desperate necessity to feel superior. In any group there are some who genuinely are superior . . . but it is easy to see that within the parameters of any group, be it culture, club, nation, profession, only a few are really superior; the mass, clearly, are not.

But it is the will of the mass that dictates the mores, initiated though changes may be by individuals or minorities; the individuals or minorities, more often than not, are cut down for their trouble. And if a unit of the mass wants to feel superior, it will find a way. This terrible drive has found expression in many ways, through history—in slavery and genocide, xenophobia and snobbery, race prejudice and sex differentiation. Given a man who, among his fellows, has no real superiority, you are faced with a bedevilled madman who, if superiority is denied him, and he cannot learn one or earn one, will turn on something weaker than himself and *make it inferior*. The obvious, logical, handiest subject for this inexcusable indignity is his woman.

If, loving, he could not have insulted this close, so-little-different other half of himself, he could never have done it to his fellow man. Without this force in him, he could never have warred, nor persecuted, nor in pursuit of superiority lied, cheated, murdered and stolen. It may be that the necessity to feel superior is the source of his drive, and his warring and killing have brought him to mighty places; yet it is not unconceivable that without it he might have turned to conquering his environment and learning his own nature, rising very much higher and, in the process, earning life for himself instead of extinction.

And strangely enough, man always wanted to love. Right up to the end, it was idiomatic that one "loved" music, a color, mathematics, a certain food—and aside from careless idiom, there were those who in the highest sense loved things beyond anything which even a fool would call sexual. "I could not love thee, dear, so much, loved I not honor more." "For God so loved the world, he gave his only begotten son . . ." Sexual love is love, certainly. But it is more precise to say that it is *loving*, in the same way we might say that justice is loving, and mercy is loving, forbearance, forgiveness, and, where it is not done to maximize the self, generosity.

Christianity was, at the outset, a love movement, as the slightest acquaintance with the New Testament clearly documents. What was not generally known until just before the end—so fiercely was all knowledge of primitive Christianity suppressed—was that it was a charitic religion—that is, a religion in which the congregation participated, in the hope of having a genuine religious experience, an experience later called theolepsy, or seized of God.

Many of the early Christians did achieve this state, and often; many more achieved it but seldom, and yet kept going back and back seeking it. But once having experienced it, they were profoundly changed, inwardly gratified; it was this intense experience, and its permanent effects, which made it possible for them to endure the most frightful hardships and tortures, to die gladly, to fear nothing.

Few dispassionate descriptions of their services—gatherings is a better term—survive, but the best accounts agree on a picture of people slipping away from fields, shops, even palaces, to be together in some hidden place—a mountain glade, a catacomb, anywhere where they might be uninterrupted. It is significant that rich and poor alike mingled at these gatherings: male and female. After eating together—genuinely, a love feast—and invoking the spirit, perhaps by song, and very likely by the dance, one or another might be seized by what they called the Spirit. Perhaps he or she—and it might be either—would exhort and praise God, and perhaps the true charitic (that is, divinely gifted) expression would issue forth in what was called "speaking in tongues," but these exhibitions, when genuine, were apparently not excessive nor frenetic; there was often time for many to take their turn. And with a kiss of peace, they would separate and slip back to their places in the world until the next meeting.

The primitive Christians did not invent charitic religion, by any means; nor did it cease with them. It recurs again and again throughout recorded history, and it takes many forms. Frequently they are orgiastic, Dionysic, like the worship of the Great Mother of the Gods, Cybele, which exerted an immense influence in Rome, Greece and the Orient a thousand years before Christ. Or chastity-based movements like the Cathars of the Middle Ages, the Adamites, the Brethren of the Free Spirit, the Waldenses (who tried to bring a form of apostolic Christianity into the framework of the Roman church) and many, many others appear all through history. They have in common one element—the subjective, participant, ecstatic experience—and almost invariably the equality of women, and they are all love religions.

Without exception they were savagely persecuted.

It seems that there is a commanding element in the human makeup which regards loving as anathema, and will not suffer it to live.

Why?

An objective examination of basic motivations (and Charlie! I *know* you can't be objective! but bear with this!) reveals the simple and terrible reason.

There are two direct channels into the unconscious mind. Sex is one, religion is the other; and in pre-Christian times, it was usual to express them together. The Judeo-Christian system put a stop to it, for a very understandable reason. *A charitic religion interposes nothing between the worshipper and his Divinity.* A suppliant, suffused with worship, speaking in tongues, his whole body in the throes of ecstatic dance, is not splitting doctrinal hairs nor begging intercession from temporal or literary authorities. As to his conduct between times, his guide is simple. He will seek to do that which will make it possible to repeat the experience. If he does what for him is right in this endeavor, he will repeat it; if he is not able to repeat it, that alone is his total and complete punishment.

He is guiltless.

The only conceivable way to use the immense power of innate religiosity—the need to worship—for the acquistion of human power, is to place between worshipper and Divinity a guilt mechanism. The only way to achieve that is to organize and systematize worship, and the obvious way to bring this about is to monitor that other great striving of life—sex.

Homo sapiens is unique among species, extant and extinct, in having devised systems for the suppression of sex.

There are only three ways of dealing with sex. It may be gratified; it may be repressed; or it may be sublimated. The latter is, through history, often an ideal and frequently a success, but it is *always* an instability. Simple, day-by-day gratification, as in what is called the Golden Age of Greece, where they instituted three classes of women: wives, *hetaerae* and prostitutes, and at the same time idealized homosexuality, may be barbaric and immoral by many standards, but produces a surprising degree of sanity. A careful look, on the other hand, at the Middle Ages, makes the mind reel; it is like opening a window on a vast insane asylum, as broad as the world and as long as a thousand years; here is the product of repression. Here are the scourging manias, when people by the thousands flogged themselves and each other from town to town, seeking penance from excesses of guilt; here is the mystic Suso, in the fourteenth century, who had made for him an undergarment for his loins, bearing a hundred and fifty brass nails filed sharp; and lest he try to ease himself in his sleep, a leather harness to hold his wrists firmly against his neck; and further, lest he try to relieve himself of the lice and fleas which plagued him, he put on leather gloves studded with sharp nails which would tear his flesh wherever he touched it; and touch it he did, and when the wounds healed he tore them open again. He lay upon a discarded wooden door with a nail-studded cross against his back, and in forty years he never took a bath. Here are saints licking out lepers' sores; here is the Inquisition.

All this in the name of love.

How could such a thing so change?

The examination of one sequence clearly shows how. Take the suppression of the Agape, the "love feast," which seems to have been a universal and necessary appurtenance of primitive Christianity. It can be unearthed by records of edicts against this and that practice, and it is significant that the elimination of a rite so important to worship seems to have taken between three and four hundred years to accomplish, and was done by a gradualism of astonishing skill and efficiency.

First of all, the Eucharist, the symbolic ritual of the body and blood of Christ, was introduced into the Agape. Next, we find the Agape better organized; there is now a bishop, without whom the Agape may not be held, for he must bless the food. A little later the bishop is traditionally kept standing through the meal, which of course keeps him separate, and above the others. After that, the kiss of peace is altered; instead of kissing one another, all the participants kiss the officiating priest and later, they all kiss a piece of wood which is handed around and passed to the priest. And then, of course, the kiss is done away with altogether. In the year 363, the Council of Laodicaea is able to establish the Eucharist as a major ritual by itself, by forbidding the Agape within a church, thus separating them. For many years the Agape was held outside the church door, but by 692 (the Trullan Council) it was possible to forbid it altogether, under the penalty of excommunication.

The Renaissance cured many of the forms of insanity, but not the insanity itself. When temporal and ecclesiastical authorities still maintained control over basically sexual matters—morals, and marriage, for example (although it was very late in the game when the Church actually performed marriage; marriages in England at the time of Shakespeare were by private contract valid, and by Church blessing licit) guilt was still rife, guilt was still the filter between a man and his God. Love was still equated with passion and passion with sin, so that at one point it was held to be sinful for a man to love his wife with passion. Pleasure, the outer edge of ecstasy, was in the dour days of Protestantism, considered sinful in itself, wherever gained; Rome held specifically that any or all sexual pleasure was sinful. And for all this capped volcano produced in terms of bridges and houses, factories and bombs, it gouted from its riven sides a frightful harvest of neurosis. And even where a nation officially discarded the church, the same repressive techniques remained, the same preoccupation with doctrine, filtered through the same mesh of guilt. So sex and religion, the real meaning of human existence, ceased to be meaning and became means; the unbridgeable hostility between the final combatants was the proof of the identity of their aim—the total domination, for the ultimate satisfaction of the will to superiority, of all human minds.

HERB RAILE GOES IN TO SAY GOODNIGHT TO THE KIDS. HE KNEELS on the floor by Karen's bed. Davy watches. Herb cradles Karen in his arms, tickles her tummy until she squeals, kisses the side of her neck and bites the lobe of her ear. Davy watches, big-eyed. Herb covers Karen's head with the blanket, quickly ducks out of sight so she can't see him when she pulls the blanket down. She searches, finds him, giggles wildly. He kisses her again, smooths the blanket over her, whispers "Your daddy *loves* you," says goodnight and turns to Davy, who watches, solemn.

Herb reaches out his right hand. Davy takes it. Herb shakes it. "Good night, old man," he says. He releases the hand. "Good night, Dad," says Davy, not looking at Herb. Herb turns out the light and leaves. Davy gets out of bed, wads up his pillow, crosses the room and whangs the pillow down as hard as he can on Karen's face.

"I can't," says Herb quite a while later, after the tears are dried and the recriminations done with, "understand whatever made him do that."

We Ledom renounce the past.

We Ledom (continued the cerebrostyle "letter") leave the past forever, and all products of the past except for naked and essential humanity.

The special circumstances of our birth make this possible. We come from a nameless mountain and as a species we are unique; as all species, we are transient. Our transience is our central devotion. Transience is passage, is dynamism, is movement, is change, is evolution, is mutation, is life.

The special circumstance of our birth includes the blessed fact that in the germ-plasm is no indoctrination. Had homo sap. had the sense (it had the power) it could have shut off all its poisons, vanquished all its dangers, by raising one clean new generation. Had homo sap. had the desire (it had both sense and power enough) to establish a charitic religion and a culture to harmonize with it, it would in time have had its clean generations.

Homo sap. claimed to be searching for a formula to end its woes. Here is the formula: a charitic religion and a culture to go with it. The Apostles of Jesus found it. Before them the Greeks found it; before them, the Minoans. Since then the Cathars found it, the Quakers, the Angel Dancers. Throughout the Orient and in Africa it had been found repeatedly ... and each time it has failed to move any but those it touched directly. Men—or at least, the men who moved men—always found that the charitic is intolerant of doctrine, neither wanting it nor needing it. But without doctrine—presbyter, interpreter, officiator—the men who move men are powerless—that is to say, not superior. There is nothing to gain in charistism.

Except, of course, the knowledge of the soul; and everlasting life.

Father-dominated people who form father-dominated cultures have father-religions: a male deity, an authoritative scripture, a strong central government, an intolerance for inquiry and research, a repressive sexual attitude, a deep conservatism (for one does not change what Father built), a rigid demarcation, in dress and conduct, between the sexes, and a profound horror of homosexuality.

Mother-dominated people who form mother-dominated cultures have mother-religions: a female deity served by priestesses, a liberal government—one which feeds the masses and succors the helpless—a great tolerance for experimental thought, a permissive attitude toward sex, a hazy boundary between the insignes of the sexes, and a dread of incest.

The father-dominated culture seeks always to impose itself upon others. The other does not. So it is the first, the patrist culture which tends to establish itself in the main stream, the matrist which rises within it, occasionally revolts, more often is killed. They are not stages of evolution, but phases marking swings of the pendulum.

The patrists poison themselves. The matrists tend to decay, which is merely another kind of poison. Occasionally one will meet a person who has been equally influenced by his mother and his father, and emulates the best of both. Usually, however, people fall into one category or the other; this is a slippery fence on which to walk. . . .

Except for the Ledom.

We are liberal in art and in technological research, in expression of all kinds. We are immovably conservative in certain areas: our conviction, each of us, never to lose the skills of the hand and of the land. We are raising children who will emulate neither mother-images nor father-images, but parents; and our deity is the

Child. We renounce and forgo all products of the past but ourselves, though we know there is much there that is beautiful; that is the price we pay for quarantine and health; that is the wall we put between ourselves and the dead hand. This is the only taboo, restriction—and the only demand we have from those who bore us.

For, like homo sap., we were born of earth and of the creatures of earth; we were born of a race of half-beasts, half-savages; homo sap. birthed us. Like homo sap. we are denied the names of those from whom we sprung, though, like men, we have much evidence of the probabilities. Our human parents built us a nest, and cared for us until we were fledged, but would not let us know them, because, unlike most men, they knew themselves and therefore would not be worshipped. And no one but themselves, they and the mothers, knew of us, that we were here, that we were something new on the face of earth. They would not betray us to homo sap., for we were different, and like all pack, herd, hive animals, homo sap. believes in the darkest part of the heart that whatever is different is by definition dangerous, and should be exterminated. Especially if it is similar in any important way (oh how horrible the gorilla, how contemptible the baboon) and most especially if in some way it might be superior, possessing techniques and devices surpassing their own (remember the Sputnik Reaction, Charlie?) but with absolute and deadly certainty if their sex activities fall outside certain arbitrary limits; for this is the key to all unreason, from outrage to envy. In a cannibal society it is immoral not to eat human flesh.

The stud went *chuck!* and Charlie Johns found himself looking up into Philos' sardonic smiling eyes.

He said, startled into English, "Well, for *God's* sake!"

"**N**O BOWLING TONIGHT, HONEY?"

"No, honey. I called Tillie Smith and begged off and she was glad and I was glad."

"You gals tiffing?"

"Oh, no! Far from it. It's just that . . . well, Tillie's very touchy these days. She knows it and she knows I know it. She'd much rather skip bowling altogether than get huffy with me and she knows she would if she did so she won't."

"Sounds like the old prostate acting up again!"

"Herb, you're gossiping. Besides, she hasn't got a prostate."

"She hasn't got Smitty's prostate, so that's the trouble."

"Oh, I guess so, Herb, you old scandal-monger you."

"Sex . . . it's like pants."

"Wh . . . ?—oh dear, there you go getting philosophical again. All right—get it off your chest."

"Not philosophical. More like what do you call making fables?"

"Fabulous."

"So I'm fabulous. Sex is like pants. All right. I go from here down Begonia to the Avenue and walk two blocks and get cigarettes and walk back, pass a lot of people, nobody notices."

"*Every*body notices, you great big handsome—"

"No wait—wait. Nobody really notices. You come along and ask all those people I passed, did they see me. Some say yes; most don't know. You get the ones said yes, ask 'em what type pants I was wearing. Now actually they could be chinos or dungarees or from the tux with black silk stripes or gabardine."

"This isn't about sex."

"Wait, wait. Now suppose I leave here to go to the drug store I don't wear any pants."

"*Any* pants?"

"Uh-huh. Now who notices?"

"You wouldn't get as far as the Avenue. Don't you dare try it, right past the Palmers'."

"Everybody notices—right! So—sex. Somebody get enough, it hardly even matters what kind, as long as it's not too funny-lookin', he goes about his business, don't think about it, don't bother anyone else. But when he has none, none at all, boy! From here to there, it's all he can think about, but *all*, and likewise he bothers everyone in sight. Tillie."

"Oh, *that* wouldn't bother Tillie."

"Not what I mean. I mean, that's the way with Tillie now. What's bothering her, you can't go bowling she's too jumpy."

"I think you're right, you know that, about sex is like pants. Only don't go talking it around, people will say you said Tillie doesn't wear pants." Jeanette laughs shrilly. "What a thought. Any old pants."

"Long as it covers the situation. Yuk. Something old, something new, something borrowed, something blue."

"Yuk yourself, and don't you dare try it."

O *utside in the hall they met Mielwis, who said, "How are you* coming along, Charlie Johns?"

"I'm there," said Charlie warmly. "I think you're the most remarkable thing ever to hit this old planet, you Ledom. It's enough to make a fellow really religious, the business of a mutation like you coming along just when the rest of us were going up in smoke."

"You approve of us, then."

"Once you get used to the idea . . . well, I should say I do! God, it's a pity there weren't a few of you around—ah—preaching or something. I mean it."

Mielwis and Philos exchanged a glance. "No," said Philos, as it were across Charlie and out of his range, "not yet."

"Will it be soon?"

"I think we'll go out to the Edge," said Philos. "Just Charlie and I."

"Why?" Mielwis asked.

Philos smiled, and the dark lights in his eyes flashed. "It takes a while to walk back."

Mielwis then smiled too, and nodded. "I'm glad you think well of us, Charlie Johns," he said. "I hope you always do."

"What else?" said Charlie, as he and Philos turned away down the corridor. They dropped down a shaft, and in the main court, Charlie demanded, "Now what was that all about?"

"There's still something you don't know," said Philos, waving at a child, who twinkled back at him.

"Something you're going to show me out at the Edge?"

"What I said to Mielwis," replied Philos, obviously not answering the question, "was, in effect, that after I tell you the rest of it, a good long walk might help you to shake it down."

"Is it that hard to take?" laughed Charlie.

Philos did not laugh. "It's that hard to take."

So Charlie stopped laughing, and they walked out of the Medical One and struck off across the open land in a direction new to Charlie.

"I miss the dark," said Charlie after a while, looking up at the silver sky. "The stars ... what about astronomy, Philos, and geophysics, and things like that, that need a little more scope than olive groves and farm fields?"

"There's plenty of that in the cerebrostyle files, in case it gets important suddenly. Meanwhile," said Philos, "it'll wait."

"For what?"

"For a livable world."

"How long will that be?"

Philos shrugged. "Nobody can tell yet. Seace thinks we should put up a satellite every hundred years or so to check."

"Every hundred years or so? For God's sake. Philos—how long are you going to stay bottled up here?"

"As long as it takes. Look, Charlie, mankind has spent some thousands of years looking outward. There's a great deal more in the files about the composition of white dwarf stars than there is about the structure of the earth under our feet. It's a good analogy; we need to balance things up a bit by spending a while looking inward instead of outward. As one of your writers—Wylie, I think—said, we have to get away from the examination of the *object* and get to know the *subject*."

"And meanwhile you're at a standstill!" cried Charlie, and waved an indicative hand at a distant Ledom patiently weeding with a hoe. "What are you going to do—stand still for ten thousand years?"

"What is ten thousand years," asked Philos equably, "in the history of a *race*?"

They walked in silence for a time over the rolling land, until Charlie gave a small, almost embarrassed laugh and said: "I guess I'm not used to thinking that big. . . . Listen, I'm still hazy about just how the Ledom got started."

"I know," said Philos reflectively. "Well, with the first two, word passed to a number of very intelligent and far-thinking people. As I told you in the 'style, they made it a point to conceal their identities from us, and you can be sure they were ten times as cautious with the rest of the world. Homo sap. wouldn't take kindly to the idea of being supplanted; am I right?"

"I'm afraid you are."

"Even if the new species wasn't in direct competition," nodded Philos. "Well then: though we don't have any direct knowledge as to who they were, it's clear that they must have had very astute advice in a dozen different fields. They developed the first cerebrostyle, for example, and did most of the groundwork on the A-field, though I don't think the first field was actually generated until we were on our own. Whether they worked on us—for us—until they died, or brought the work to a certain point and then sealed us off, and went back to wherever they came from, I couldn't say. I only know for certain that there was a small colony of young Ledom in a large mountain cave which opened onto an otherwise inaccessible valley. The Ledom never set foot in that valley until the A-field was developed and it could be roofed over."

"Then the air wasn't radioactive, or anything like that!"

"No, it wasn't."

"Then the Ledom actually coexisted with homo sap. for a while!"

"Yes indeed. The only way they might have been discovered would be from the air. Of course, once the A-field was ready, that was no longer a problem."

"What does it look like from the air?"

"I'm told," said Philos, "it looks like more mountains."

"Philos, you Ledom all resemble one another pretty much. Are—were you all one family?"

"Yes and no. As I understand it, there were two of us at first unrelated. The rest are descended from those."

Charlie thought a moment, then decided not to ask the question which was in his mind. Instead he asked, "Could anyone leave here?"

"No one would want to, would they?"

"But—*could* they?"

"I suppose so," said Philos, in a mildly irritated tone. Charlie wondered if this was a conditioning or some such. It would be logical. "How long have the Ledom been here?"

"I'll answer that," said Philos, "but not now."

A little taken aback, Charlie trudged along for a while in silence. Then he asked, "Are there any more Ledom settlements like this?"

"None." Philos seemed to becoming more and more laconic.

"And isn't there anyone out there at all?"

"We presume not."

"Presume? Don't you know?" When Philos would not respond, Charlie asked him point-blank, "Is homo sap. really extinct?"

"Inescapably," said Philos; and he had to be satisfied with that.

They had reached the edge of the valley, and were climbing foothills. The going was more difficult but Philos seemed to want to go faster, seemed to be driven by something. Charlie noticed how he kept examining the rocks about them, kept looking back toward the looming Ones.

"You looking for something?"

"Just a place to sit down," said Philos. They threaded their way between huge boulders and came at last to a steep slope, part solid rock, part talus. Philos glanced again toward the Ones—they were invisible from here—and said in a strange, taut voice, "Sit down."

Charlie, realizing that he had for many minutes been building up to something large, something unexpected, found himself a flat rock and crouched on it.

"This is where I . . . lost . . . my mate, my Froure," said Philos.

Recalling that he had promised Nasive that he would not admit previous knowledge, Charlie, with no difficulty at all, put a sympathetic expression on his face and said nothing.

"It was a long time ago," said Philos. "I had just been given the history assignment. The overall idea was to see what would happen if one of us was drenched with it; if it was as poisonous as some people feared. And by some people, I mean some of the people who worked with us in the First Cave. They believed pretty strongly that we should cut all ties with homo sap., who seemed to have fumbled the ball pretty badly, and try not to emulate him in any way, even unconsciously. This would cost us his art, his literature, and a great deal of what was good in his evaluations; but at the same time they did not want us denied his pure sciences— you mentioned astronomy yourself—and some of the developmental data. It pays, you know, sometimes, to know what mistakes to avoid. It not only saves trouble; in a moral sense it makes some of the most appalling errors worth while, good for something. So . . . try it on the dog first," he said, with a bitter little smile.

"I'd gotten about as far along as you are in the study of the Ledom and of homo sap., though in a good deal more detail. Froure and I had been married only a short while, and I'd had to spend a lot of time alone. I thought it would be nice if Froure and I took a long slow walk, just to talk, to be together. We were both pregnant. . . . We sat down here and the . . . the . . ." Philos swallowed and began over. "The ground opened up. That's the only way I can say it. Froure went right . . . *down*. I jumped to—"

"I'm sorry," said Charlie uselessly.

"Four days later they dug me out. They never found Froure. I lost both my babies. The only ones I'll ever have, I guess."

"But surely you could—"

Philos interrupted the warm suggestion. "But surely I wouldn't—" he said, pleasantly mocking. Seriously, then, "I like you, Charlie Johns, and I trust you. I'd like to show you why I can't possibly marry, but you'll have to promise me your absolute confidence."

"Certainly!"

Philos regarded him solemnly for a long moment, then touched his hands together. The mirror-field sprang into existence. He placed the ring, with the field still operating, on the ground, stepped back a yard, and gave a sharp pull at the edge of a flat rock. It tilted, discovering a dim hole or tunnel-mouth. The mirror, frameless and perfect, reflecting against the big boulder, would offer perfect camouflage to the hole behind it, should anyone approach from the Ones. Philos dropped into the hole, beckoned to Charlie, and passed out of sight.

Thunderstruck, Charlie followed.

T HIRTY PEOPLE IN THE LIVING ROOM IS A BIT OF A SQUEEZE, BUT it's all friendly and informal and people don't mind sprawling around on the floor. The minister is a good man. He's a good man, thinks Herb, in any old way you want to use the words. When this Rev. Bill Flester was a chaplain in the army, he'd bet the church people said that and the brass and the GI's too. Flester has clear eyes and very good teeth, and iron-grey, crew-cut hair and a young ruddy face. His clothes are sober but not funereal, and his narrow tie and narrow lapels, like his words, speak their language. He has begun by stating a thesis like a text for a sermon, but it is not a Biblical text; it is a working phrase like what you'd run across on Madison Avenue or any place; it is "There's always a way, if you can only think of it." The neighbors listen raptly. Jeanette watches the teeth. Tillie Smith watches the shoulders, which are broad, and the iron-grey crew-cut. Smitty, folded up on the end of a coffee table leans forward and with his thumb and forefinger pulls his lower lip out so you can see clear to the floor of his mouth in front of his teeth, which is the Smith semaphore for "This guy has something here."

"Now our Jewish friends," Flester is saying, with a filtered approval, "have built themselves that very pretty little temple down on Forsythia Drive, and over on the other side of the development our Catholic buddies have themselves a nice little brick chapel. Now I've done a little reading and a lot of legwork, and I find there are twenty-two different Protestant churches within ten miles of here; people from this development go to eighteen different ones, and we have at least fifteen represented right here in this room. Now nobody's going to build fifteen or twenty or twenty-two different kinds of Protestant churches here. Now the school people know what to do about small scattered outlets, and so do the grocery people. They centralize.

"It just seems to me we ought to take a leaf from their book. A church has to look to efficiency, and product appeal, and rising costs just like any other operation. In a new situation, you find new ways to do business, like the idea of driving your car into a bank, like this shopping by television they talk about in the Sunday papers. We're all Protestants and we all want to go to church right here in the neighborhood. The only thing in our way is a question of doctrine. There are a lot of folks take their doctrine pretty seriously, and let's be frank, there have been quarrels about it.

"A lot has been done with the idea of uniting churches. You give a point, I give a point, we get together. But a lot of folks figure they have gotten together by losing something. That's the way it makes some folks feel: a compromise is when everybody loses something. We don't want that here.

"I think with all respect that some folks have hold of the wrong end of the stick. There must be a way to join together where nobody loses and everybody gains. There always *is* a way if you can only think of it.

"Now what I think, and I take no credit for it because any of you people would come up with the same answer if you had yourself involved in it like I have, I think we ought to get the people in from all the different churches, on the top level; what you would call a management group, an executive group, and I think we ought to kick around the idea of a little church for all of us. But instead of fighting about which brand to stock, let's load the shelves with all the brands, you know, top quality goods from all over. You go in there to God's supermarket with a need to fill, and it's there for you, and you wheel over and take it off the shelf.

"Now just for an example of what I mean, if one of you ladies has been loyal to Del Monte brand all your life, I wouldn't want you to hide it like a secret, I wouldn't want to hire a boy to go to work and rip off all the labels, I wouldn't want you to stop using it or stop telling all your girl-friends you think that's best. I just want you to have it and use it and be happy with it. And there's going to be no quarrel between you and the market, or between you and another customer, if she wants some other brand, because that brand is going to be right there on the same kind of shelf under good lighting and a fair display.

"If we can put this proposition to—heh—management from all over, like you might say the distributors, I don't think they will fight the idea of more distribution without disturbing consumer loyalty. I think they'll get just as enthusiastic about packaging and point-of-sale merchandizing as the store management will. Here'll be management dedicated to 'service' in a new way.

"No one needs to go without anything he really needs—that's the American way. If you want your kiddies baptized by immersion, we'll have a font or pool big enough. If you want candles on the altar, fine; a Sunday is big enough to have services with them and without them. The candlesticks can be telescopic. Pictures and decorations? Put them in slots and hinges so they can be changed or slid out of sight or anything you like.

"I won't go into any more detail about it; it's *your* church and we'll set it up your way. Long as we're guided by the idea of service—and all that means is that we're not fixing to offend anybody. There are more similar ways of loving your God than different ways of loving your God, and it's high time and past time we moved along with the main currents of the American system and let our churches service us with self-service of the best kind, with plenty of parking space and a decent playground for the kiddies."

Everybody applauds.

*P*hilos *set his shoulder against the slab and it swung up and* shut. It was totally dark for a moment, and then there was a scrabbling sound and Philos unearthed a lump of coldly glowing material and set it in a cleft. "There's one more important thing for you to learn about Ledom, and in an ugly sort of way," said Philos, "you couldn't have been given a better way to learn it. Mielwis himself hasn't the slightest notion how good. Put this on." From some hidden hollow in the rock he drew a cloak; thick cobweb might describe such a material. He got a similar one and enveloped himself in the folds. Charlie, speechless, followed suit, while Philos went on, in driving, almost angry tones. "Down Froure went, and in I plunged, and when Froure dug me out—Froure with a broken foot and four broken ribs, mind you—we found ourselves in here—it's what the geologists call a chimney. It wasn't quite this tidy. Digging out was past trying. We went *in*."

He pushed past Charlie and seemed to crouch down in black shadows in the corner; then he was gone. Charlie followed, and found the black spot was a hole, a tunnel-mouth. In the dark, Philos took his hand. Charlie stumbled on the hem of the cloak and cursed. "It's too hot."

"Keep it on," Philos ordered flatly. He moved forward purposively, all but dragging Charlie, who sidled and shuffled and did his best to keep up; and all the while Philos talked, short, sharp, hurried; what he said obviously hurt him to say. "First thing I remember we were in a sort of blind cave back in here. Froure had managed some sort of light, and I felt I was turning inside out. The babies were lost then, my two. It took about three hours. The light held out, I'm . . . sorry to say. Watch your head, it's low here. . . . about six and a half months along. Good well-formed youngsters.

"Your kind of youngsters," Philos' voice came out of the dark after a long shuffling pause. "Homo sap. youngsters."

"What?"

Philos stopped in the dark and there was a scrabbling. Again from a pile of loose rubble he drew a glowing block of material and set it up. They were in a smooth-walled cave which had at one time doubtless been a pressure-bubble in the magma of a volcano. "Right here, it was," Philos nodded. "Froure tried to hide them from me. I get . . . upset when people try to hide things from me.

"We explored a bit. The whole hillside was honeycombed with these chimneys. It no longer is, by the way. We found a way back, a hole a hundred feet away from the rock-fall. But we found a way through, too—right through the hill, and it comes out past the 'sky.'

"I was hurt and grieved and more than a little angry. Froure too. We had a crazy idea. Froure's foot and ribs were only painful, not dangerous, and we Ledom can handle pain pretty well. But I had internal injuries and something had to be done about it. So we agreed that I should go back, and Froure would just—disappear for a while."

"Why?"

"I had to find out. I'd lost two babies, and they were homo sap. Was it just me? Well, there was a way to find out. And if I found out what I was afraid of finding out, I wanted Froure and me away from Ledom—far enough, at least to be able to think it through . . .

"So I'd go back. Froure would stay. I'd get treatment, and hurry back as quickly as I could. Well . . . I crawled up the other chimney and we made another rock-fall, and the searchers found me all right, and they naturally dug where I told them, and naturally Froure was not found. But we made that second rock-fall a little too good. I was hurt again . . . it was longer, much longer, than I thought it would be when at last I was on my feet again. I hurried back here—they were oh, so understanding, and left me to grieve any way I wanted to—I hurried back, hoping against hope that I would be in time, and I was not in time. Froure, all alone, bore two babies, and one died.

"They were homo sap."

"Philos!"

"Yes, homo sap. So we began to be sure. Somehow a baby had to be born in the Medical One to be born a Ledom. Does that sound like anything you ever heard about a mutation?"

"It sure doesn't."

"There is no mutation, Charlie, and that's what Mielwis wanted you to know. And Froure is alive and here, and so is my homo sap. child, and that's what *I* wanted you to know."

It was too much—much too much—for Charlie Johns to grasp all at once. He began to take it in little bites.

"Mielwis doesn't know this happened to you."

"Right."

"Your . . . Froure is here, alive?" (But Nasive said the rock-fall had been years ago!) "How long, Philos?"

"Years. Soutin—the child—he's almost as big as you are."

"But . . . why? Why? Cutting yourselves off from everyone—"

"Charlie, as soon as I could, I began finding out all I could about Ledom—things I'd never thought to ask before. The Ledom are an open and honest people—you know that—but they're human and they need privacy. Maybe that's the way they get it—they answer questions but they do not always volunteer. There are secrets in the Medical One and the Science One—not secrets in the sense of your ridiculous 'classified' and 'restricted' and 'top secret' nonsense. But things, many things, that ordinarily it would never occur to anyone to ask about. No one ever thought to question total anesthesia for our monthly physical, for example, and we have that all our lives; no one wondered why our babies were 'incubated' for a month before we ever saw them; who would think to ask about such a thing as experimentation in time travel? Why, it was almost an accident I stumbled across the Control Natural—as it was, I never saw him—and I'd have passed by the hint if it hadn't been for Soutin's birth."

"What's the Control Natural?"

"A child hidden away in the Medical One. A homo sap. with his mind kept asleep; something they can check their work against. So you see our three that died, and Soutin, weren't the only homo saps. born here. It was when I found out about the Control Natural that we decided Soutin would stay hidden here—which of course meant Froure stayed too. When Soutin was born, he was a funny-looking little tyke—you'll forgive me, Charlie, but to us he was funny-looking—but we loved him. Everything that happened made us cherish him the more. Mielwis is never going to get Soutin."

"But . . . what's going to happen? What are you going to do?"

"That's up to you, Charlie."

"Me!"

"Will you take him back with you, Charlie?"

Charlie Johns peered through the dim silver light at the cloaked figure, the mobile, sensitive face. He thought about the doggedness, the pain, the care; the aching loneliness between two of these loving people forced to be so often apart, and all for the love they bore for their child. And he thought of the child—here a hermit-person, buried like a mole; in Ledom a freak or a laboratory animal; and back in his time—what? Without knowing the language, the customs . . . it could be worse than anything Mielwis could do.

He almost shook his head, but he couldn't, with the tearing anxiety showing on Philos' face. Besides—Seace wouldn't allow it; Mielwis wouldn't allow it. (But remember—remember? He knew the settings for the machine, remember?)

"Philos . . . could you get us to the time machine in the Science One without anyone knowing?"

"I could if I needed to."

"You need to. I'll take him."

What Philos said was nothing special. The way he said it was one of the richest rewards Charlie Johns had ever known. With his dark eyes shining, Philos merely whispered, "Let's go tell Froure and Soutin."

Philos wrapped up snugly in the thick cloak, signalling Charlie to do the same, and then placed his hands flat on the far wall, one above the other. His fingers sank into hidden purchases, and he pulled outward. A section of the smooth rock, tall as a man, rotated into the chamber. It was hollow, and shaped in cross-section like a wedge of pie. From its triangular dark interior came a gout of frosty air. "A kind of airlock," said Philos. "The 'sky' ends back there; actually, we're outside of it now. I can't just keep an open tunnel or the constant air loss would make someone curious at the pressure station." It was Charlie's first recognition that the warm, fresh air all over Ledom was not only conditioned, but pressurized as well.

"Is it winter now?"

"No, but it's almighty high up. . . . I'll go first and wait to guide you." He stepped into the wedge-shaped chamber and pressed against the inner wall. It rotated him out of sight, then swung back inside, empty. Charlie stepped in and pushed. Before him, the door-edge swung against solid rock; behind, it clipped at his heels as he pushed. And then he was standing on a hillside, under stars; he gasped from the thin sharp cold, but perhaps the gasp was more for the stars.

In the starlight, which was quite bright enough, they sprinted down the slope, dropped panting into a deep cleft in the rock, and in it, Philos found a door. He pushed it inward; warm wind blew on them. They stepped inside, and the wind blew the door shut. They went forward again, and opened a second door, and there, running toward them down a long low room, with a real wood fire cracking on a real stone hearth; running toward them gladly came Froure, limping but running, and running freely and gladly, Soutin

Charlie Johns murmured a single word and pitched forward in a dead faint; and the word he said was "Laura."

"**S**OMETIMES WHEN YOU LOOK AROUND YOU IT SCARES YOU," says Herb.

Jeanette is dipping popcorn in puddles of egg color in a muffin tin, so Davy can make himself an Indian necklace. Davy is only five but he is very good with a needle and thread. "So don't look around. What are you looking at?"

"The radio, listen to that." A voice is wailing in song. The discerning ear, if forced to listen (if not forced, the discerning ear would not listen) might recognize the theme as "Vesti la Giubba"; the lyric has to do with disappointment at the junior prom, and both lyric and theme are occluded by a piano playing octaves in the high treble: *Klingklingkling-Klingklingkling,* six quarter-notes to the measure. "Who's that singing?"

"*I* don't know," says Jeanette with a certain degree of annoyance. "I can't be bothered with all this Somebody Brothers and Miltown Trios. They all sound alike."

"Yeah, but who, who's that?"

She poises popcorn over the purple and stops to listen. "It's that wall-eyed one night before last on television with the crooked teeth," she guesses.

"No!" he says triumphantly. "That was the backstreet Fauntleroy they call Debsie. Namely a boy type. *This* is a woman, girl type."

"You don't say." She listens while the voice glisses up the entire four-and-a-half-tone compass of its range and disappears behind the tire-chain-style piano-playing. "You know, you're right."

"I know I'm right, and it scares you." Herb slaps the magazine he has been reading. "I'm reading in here where Al Capp, you know, the cartoon Al Capp, says about magazine illustrating, at long last you can tell again in a magazine illustration which is the man and which is the woman. The prettiest one is the man. So just while I'm reading that along comes the radio and there's a girl singer with that special growl that makes her sound like a boy singer sounding like a girl."

"And that scares you?"

"Well things could get confusing" he says jocosely. "Goes on like this much longer, there's going to be a mutation, that like breeds true and you don't know is a boy or a girl."

"Silly. You don't make mutations that way."

"I know it. All I mean is, things go on this way, when the double-sex type mutation arrives, nobody'll notice it."

"Oh, you're making too much of it, Herb."

"Sure. But all the same and seriously, don't you have the feeling sometimes that there's some great force at work trying to make women into men and verse vicey? Not only this singer bit. Look at Soviet Russia. Never on earth has a great social experiment turned so many women into so huge a herd of pit ponies. Look at Red China, where at last the little China dolls have been liberated out of the slavery of the honky-tonks and get to wear overalls and shovel coal fourteen hours a day alongside their brothers. It's just the other side of that record we just heard."

Jeanette dips the purple and drips it. "Oh no," she says, "on the other side is *Stardust*."

"**Y**ou said '*Laura*,' and—"

Charlie looked up at the beamed ceiling. "I'm sorry," he said faintly. "Maybe I've been too long without sleep. I'm sorry."

"What is a Laura?"

Charlie sat up, Philos assisting. He looked at the speaker, a brown-haired, grey-eyed Ledom with strong but fine-drawn features, and those rare, firm, sculptured lips which yet can smile readily. "Laura was the one I loved," he said, simply as a Ledom might say it. "You must be Froure." And then he looked again, looked again at the other.

Shy, yet standing beside, not behind, the pillar which held the beam which held the rock ceiling. Cloaked, high-collared in the Ledom manner, with biostatic material drawn like his own, snug over the breast. But then cut down and back, leaving the lower body bare but for the sporran-like silk. A face ... a *nice* face, neither boyish nor too beautiful; and oh, it was not Laura; it's just that she had Laura's hair.

She.

"Soutin," said Philos.

"Y-y-you kept saying *he!*" cried Charlie stupidly,

"About Soutin? Yes, of course—what else?"

And it came to Charlie, yes of course—what else! For Philos had told his story in the Ledom tongue, and he had always used the Ledom pronoun which is not masculine nor feminine but which also is not "it"; it was he, Charlie himself, who had translated it "he."

He said to the girl, "You have hair just like Laura's."

She said, shyly, "I'm glad you came."

They wouldn't let him sleep—they couldn't; they had not the time—but they rested and fed him; Philos and Froure toured the house, half underground, half on the rim of a high mesa, inaccessible to any wingless thing, with broad acres of woodland behind, and meadowland where, they told him, Soutin had shot deer with a bow and arrow. Philos and Froure toured the house openly, they wept, they were prepared never to see it again. It was as late as this that Charlie found himself wondering what would become of them after he had taken Soutin away. What was the thing they were doing—treason? What was the penalty for treason? He could not ask. The language had no words for concepts like punishment.

They left the house, climbed the hill, entered the airlock. Inside, they buried the block of light. Through the tunnel into the chimney-top, and there they buried the other block. They discarded their cloaks there and hid them, and came out into the green land, under the steely sky of Ledom. Slowly they walked toward the Ones, two by two like lovers, for Philos and Froure were lovers and Charlie and Soutin must walk so, for she was terrified.

Nearing the Medical One, Froure dropped back and walked with Soutin and Charlie, while Philos walked ahead. Some few might remember Froure, but not seeing him alone. But if Philos, the solitary one, were seen walking like a lover—

And all the way, holding Soutin, whispering warnings and encouragements and sometimes direct orders; all the way, the thoughts curled and burned in the back of Charlie's mind.

"Don't scream," he said to Soutin sternly as they approached the subway; he wished he had had someone to say that to him when he first saw it. Stepping into the dark entrance, he turned and caught her tight in his arms, forced her face into the cup of his shoulder. She was lithe as a lioness but as they dropped, rigid with terror. Scream! Why—she couldn't breathe!

And on the subway she simply held him; bruised him with her hard slim fingers, as she stood with eyes and lips sealed. But at the other end, when the invisible lift whisked her up, and she had her first experience of the motion that had so thoroughly destomached him—she laughed!

... And he was glad of her, parting him now and now again from the thoughts

—of love one another

—of man with grafted uterus coupling with man with grafted uterus

—of the knowing pride of children, worshipped

—of the hand of Grocid, and of Nasive, in burnished wood

—of the knives and needles stitching a manmade and inhuman newness into the bodies of babes

—and oh the distance between, or the fusion of,

deity and a dirty joke.

They flung up the side of the tilting structure. Charlie smothering Soutin's wild laughter in his shoulder, and walked into the bright shuttered silence of Seace's laboratory. *He won't be there,* Charlie told himself urgently.

But he was there. He turned from some equipment at the end of the room and strode toward them, unsmiling.

Charlie sidled, drawing Soutin with him, making it necessary for Seace to pass him in order to speak to Philos.

Seace said, "Philos, it is not your time to be here."

Philos, pale, opened his mouth to speak, when *"Seace!"* cried Froure sharply.

Seace had not seen Froure, or had not looked at the long "dead" Ledom. He turned to brush away the interruption, and then his gaze snapped, clamped, clung to Froure's fine-drawn features. Froure smiled and touched his hands together, and the mirror-field sprang out; it was fiendish, it was exquisite in timing, for the scientist, given one clear glimpse of that unmistakable face, impossibly here and living, saw it replaced with his own image. At the very moment he was doubting his eyes, his eyes were denied him.

"Take it down," he said hoarsely. "Froure: is it Froure?" He came breathing up to the intangible plane of the mirror; Philos slipped beside Froure and took the ring; Froure slipped aside and Philos played Seace up the room like a hypnotized bird, then snapped it off and stood smiling. *"Seace!"* called Froure from behind him. . . .

And all the while Charlie Johns was working, working at the control dials of the time machine. He set them, one, two, three, four, thumbed the toggle, turned and flung Soutin through the open door of the machine, dove after her, hooking the door to in midair as he dove. The last thing he saw as the door swung was Seace, aware at last, flinging Froure roughly aside, leaping for the controls.

Charlie and Soutin fell together in a tangle. For a moment they stayed just as they were, and then Charlie got to his feet, knelt by the trembling girl, and put his arms around her.

"I wanted to say good-bye to them," she whispered.

"It's going to be all right," he soothed. He stroked her hair. Suddenly—perhaps it was reaction—he laughed. "Look at us!"

She did: at him, at herself, and turned frightened attentive eyes to him. He said, "I was thinking what it will be like, on the stairs, when we arrive; me in the Superman outfit, you . . ."

She pulled at her high-collared, swept-back garment. "I won't know what to do. I'm so . . ." She moved the silk of her "sporran." "This," she said, her voice cracking with the desperate courage of confessional, "it isn't real; I couldn't ever grow . . . Do you suppose they'll know, where we're going?"

He stopped laughing instantly. "They'll never know," he assured her soberly.

"I'm so frightened," she said.

"You never need to be frightened again," he told her. Nor I, he thought. Philos wouldn't have sent her back to the time when humanity lit the fuse. Or . . . would he? Would he think it worth while to give her a year among her own kind, a month, even if she must die with them?

He wished he could ask Philos.

She said, "How long will it take?"

He glanced at the hairline crack which was the door. "I don't know. Seace said, instantaneous . . . from the Ledom end. I suppose," he said, "the door wouldn't open while the machine is . . ." he was going to say "moving" and then "traveling" and then "operating" and they all seemed wrong. "I guess if the door is unlocked, we'll have arrived."

"Are you going to try it?"

"Sure," he said. He didn't go near it, or look at it.

"Don't be frightened," she said.

Charlie Johns turned and opened the door.

"GOD BLESS MOMMY AND DADDY AND GRANDMA SAL AND Grandma Felix and I guess Davy too," sings Karen to her own tune. "And—"

"Go on, dear. Was there someone else?"

"Mmm. And God bless God, ay-men."

"Well, that's very sweet, dear. But why?"

Karen says through the translucent margins of slumber, "I just always God-bless everybody that loves me, that's why."

Charlie Johns opened the door into a blaze of light, a blaze of silver light, a silver blaze of overcast, a stretch of silver from here clear to the Medical One, point-down and tipped and filling the view.

"You forgot something," said a voice. Mielwis.

Behind Charlie, a stricken sound. Not turning, "Stay where you are!" he rapped. Instantly Soutin pushed past him, ran out of the machine, by the controls, by Mielwis, by Grocid, by Nasive, by Seace, all of whom stared at her while she flung herself down beside Philos and Froure, who lay side by side on the floor, their hands flat and neat on their abdomens, their feet too limp. For a moment nothing was heard but Soutin's hard inhalations; the sighs between were silent.

"If you've killed them," Charlie said at last, in a voice full of hate, "You've killed their child too."

There was no comment, unless Nasive's dropped gaze was a comment. Mielwis said softly, "Well?" Charlie knew he was referring to his earlier remark.

"I forgot nothing. I appointed Philos to report to you. As far as I made any promises at all, I kept them that way."

"Philos is unable to report."

"That's your doing. What about your end of the deal?"

"We keep our promises."

"Let's get to it."

"We want your reactions to Ledom first."

What can I lose now? he thought forlornly, but there was no softening in him. He slitted his eyes and said carefully, "You're the rottenest pack of perverts that ever had the good sense to hide in a hole."

A sort of rustle went through them—movement, not sound. Finally, "What changed you, Charlie Johns? You thought very well of us a few hours ago. What changed you?"

"Only the truth."

"What truth?"

"That there is no mutation."

"Our doing it ourselves makes that much difference? Why is what we have done worse to you than a genetic accident?"

"Just because you do it." Charlie heaved a deep breath, and almost spit as he said, "Philos told me how old a people you are. Why is what you do evil? Men marrying men. Incest, perversion, there isn't anything rotten you don't do."

"Do you think," said Mielwis courteously, "that your attitude is unusual, or would be if the bulk of mankind had your information?"

"About a hundred and two percent unanimous," Charlie growled.

"Yet a mutation would have made us innocent."

"A mutation would have been natural. Can you say that about yourself?"

"Yes! Can you? Can homo sap.? Are there degrees of 'nature'? What is it about a gene-changing random cosmic particle that is more natural than the force of the human mind?"

"The cosmic ray obeys the laws of nature. You're abrogating them."

"It was homo sap. who abrogated the law of the survival of the fittest," said Mielwis soberly. "Tell me, Charlie Johns: what would homo sap. do if we shared the world with them and they knew our secrets?"

"We'd exterminate you down to the last queer kid," said Charlie coldly, "and stick that one in a side-show. That's all I have to say. Get me out of here."

Mielwis sighed. Nasive said suddenly, "All right, Mielwis. You were right."

"Nasive has held all along that we should share ourselves and the A-field and the cerebrostyle with homo sap. I feel you would try to do as you just said—and that you'd turn the field into a weapon and the 'style into a device for the enslavement of minds."

"We probably would, to wipe you off the earth. Now crank up your time machine."

"There isn't any time machine."

Literally, Charlie's knees buckled. He turned and looked at the great silver sphere.

"*You* said it was a time machine. We didn't. You told Philos it was—he believed you."

"Seace—"

"Seace arranged some scenery. A watch with backwards numerals. A book of matches. But it was you—you who believed what you wanted to believe. You do that, you homo sap. You let anyone help you, if he helps you believe what you want to believe."

"You said you'd send me back!"

"I said we'd return you to your previous state, and we will."

"You . . . *used* me!"

Mielwis nodded, almost cheerfully.

"Get me out of this," snarled Charlie. "Whatever you're gibbering about." He pointed to the grieving girl. "I want Soutin as well. You've gotten along fine without Soutin so far."

"I think that would be fair," said Grocid.

"How soon do you want to—"

"Now! Now! Now!"

"Very well." Mielwis held up a hand; somehow it made everyone stop breathing. Mielwis spoke a two-syllable word: "Quesbu."

Charlie Johns shuddered from head to foot, and slowly put up his hands and covered his eyes.

After a time, Mielwis said softly, "Who are you?"

Charlie put down his hands. "Quesbu."

"Don't be alarmed, Quesbu. You're yourself again. Don't be afraid anymore."

Grocid, awed, breathed, "I didn't think it could be done."

Seace said rapidly, softly, "His own name—a posthypnotic command. He's really—but Mielwis will explain."

Mielwis spoke: "Quesbu: do you still remember the thoughts of Charlie Johns?"

The man who had been Charlie Johns said dazedly, "Like . . . a sort of dream or . . . or a story someone told."

"Come here, Quesbu."

Trusting, childlike, Quesbu came. Mielwis took his hand, and against the young man's biceps he pressed a white sphere, which collapsed. Without a sound Quesbu collapsed. Mielwis caught him deftly and carried him over to the side, where Philos and Froure lay. He put Quesbu down beside them and looked into the frightened, lost eyes of Soutin.

"It's all right, little one," Mielwis whispered. "They're only resting. Soon you'll be together again." He moved slowly, so as not to startle her, but with great sureness, and touched her with another of the little spheres.

ꓚEANETTE TELLS HERB ABOUT KAREN: SHE SAYS GOD BLESS GOD, because she God-blesses everybody who loves her.

"So does God," says Herb flippantly; and as the words hang there it is not flippant any more.

"I *love* you," says Jeanette.

*A*nd at last the heads of Ledom may confer quietly among themselves.

"But there really was a Charlie Johns?" asked Nasive.

"Oh yes indeed there was."

"It's . . . not a happy thing," said Nasive. "When I took the position that we should share what we have with homo sap., it was a . . . sort of unreal argument. There wasn't anything real involved, somehow; just words, just names of things." He sighed. "I liked him. He seemed to—to understand things, like our statue, *The Maker*, yes, and the feast . . ."

"He understood all right," said Seace with a touch of sarcasm. "I'd like to have seen how much he understood if we'd told him the truth about ourselves before he saw the statue and the feast, instead of afterward."

"Who was he, Mielwis?"

Mielwis exchanged a look with Seace, shrugged slightly, and answered, "I might as well tell you. He was in a homo sap. flying machine that crashed in the mountains near here. It came apart in the air. Most of it burned and fell on the other side, far away. But that one part landed right on our 'sky' and perched there. Charlie Johns was inside, very badly hurt, and another homo sap. who was already dead. Now, you know the 'sky' looks just like mountains from above, but all the same it wouldn't be too good an idea to have search parties climbing around on it.

"Seace saw the wreckage up there in his instruments, and immediately put up an A-field carrier and snatched it down. I did my very best to save his life, but he was too badly hurt. He never regained consciousness. But I did manage to get a complete cerebrostyle record of his mind."

Seace said, "It's the most complete record we ever got of a mind."

"Then it came to us, Seace and me, that we could use the record to find out what homo sap. would think of us if he knew about us. All we had to do was to suppress the id, the 'me' part of someone by deep hypnosis, and replace it with Charlie Johns' cerebrostyle record. Having Quesbu, it was a simple matter."

Grocid wagged his head in amazement. "We didn't even *know* about Quesbu."

"The Control Natural. No, you wouldn't. A research property of the Medical One. There has never been any reason to tell anyone about Quesbu. He's been well-treated—happy, even, I think, though he's never known anything but his own compound in the Medical One."

"He has now," said Nasive.

Grocid asked, "What's to become of them—Quesbu and the other?"

Mielwis smiled. "If it hadn't been for this incredible Philos and his hiding Froure and the child all these years—and hide them he did; I never in the world suspected a thing about it—I'd be hard put to it to answer that. Quesbu could hardly be confined again, after his stretch as Charlie Johns, even if he regards it as a dream. For a lot of his experience wasn't dream at all—he did, after all, personally and truly visit all the Ones. Yet he's too old now to be turned into a Ledom, except in a partial way; I wouldn't commit such a thing upon him.

"But the child Soutin gives us a new opportunity. Can you imagine what it might be?"

Grocid and Nasive shared a glance. "We could build them a house?"

Mielwis shook his head. "Not in the Children's One," he said positively. "They're too . . . different. Any amount of care, of love, even, couldn't make up for it. It would be asking too much of them, and perhaps too much of us. Never forget who we are, Grocid—what we are, what we're for. Humanity has never attained its optimum ability to reason, its maximum objectivity, until now, because it has always plagued itself with its dichotomies. In us, the very concept of any but individual differences has been eliminated. And Quesbu and Soutin are not different in an individual sense; they are a different *kind*. We Ledom could probably cope with it better than they, but we are still new, young, unpracticed; we are only in our fourth generation . . ."

"Really?" said Nasive. "I thought . . . I mean, I *didn't* think. I didn't know."

"Few of us know; few of us care, because it doesn't matter. We are conditioned to look ahead, not back. But because it bears on our decision of what to do with Quesbu and Soutin, I'll tell you briefly how the Ledom came to be.

"It has to be brief; for we know so little . . .

"There was a homo sap., a very great one; whether he was known as such among his kind, I do not know. It seems probable that he was. I think he was a physiologist or a surgeon; he must have been both, and a great deal more. He was sickened by mankind, not so much for the evils it committed, but because of the good in itself it was destroying. It came to him that humankind, having for some thousands of years enslaved itself, was inescapably about to destroy itself, unless a society could be established which would be above all the partisanship which had divided it, and unless this society could be imbued with a loyalty to nothing but humanity.

"He may have worked alone for a long time; I know that at the end, he was joined by a number of like-thinking people. His name, their names, are not known; humanity honors by emulating, and he wished us to copy nothing from homo sap. that could be avoided.

"He and his friends made us, designed our way of life; gave us our religion and the cerebrostyle and the rudiments of the A-field, and helped the first generation to maturity."

Nasive said suddenly, "Then some of us must have known them!"

Mielwis shrugged. "I suppose so. But what did they know? They dressed, acted, spoke like Ledom; one by one they died or disappeared. As an infant, a child, you accept what you see around you. We four are teachers—right? So were they.

"And all they ever asked of us was that we keep humanity alive. Not their art, music, literature, architecture. Them*selves;* in the widest sense, the self of humanity.

"We are not really a species. We are a biological 'construct.' In a cold-blooded way we might be called a kind of machine with a function. The function is to keep humanity alive while it is murdered, and after it is well dead—

"To give it back!

"And that is the one aspect of Ledom which we never told Charlie Johns, because he would never believe it. No homo sap. would or could. Virtually never in human history has a group in power had the wisdom to abdicate, to relinquish, except under pressure.

"We are to be as we are, stay as we are, keeping the skills of the soil, holding open the two great roads to the inner self—religion, and love—and studying humanity as humanity has never troubled to study before—from the outside in. And from time to time we must meet with homo sap. to see if he is yet ready to live, to love, and to worship without the crutch of implanted bi-sexuality. When he is—and he will be if it takes us ten thousand, or fifty thousand years, we the Ledom will simply cease. We are not a Utopia. A Utopia is something finished, completed. We are transients; custodians; a bridge, if you like.

"The pure accident of Charlie Johns' arrival here gave us an opportunity to find out how homo sap. would react to the idea of the Ledom. You saw what happened. But the factor of Soutin, now: that presents us with a new opportunity, and our very first to see if homo sap. can be made ready for its own maturity."

"Mielwis! You mean to set them out to start a new—"

"Not a new homo sap. The old one, with a chance to live without hate. To live, like all young things, with a hand to guide them."

Grocid and Nasive smiled at one another. "Our specialty."

Mielwis smiled back, but shook his head. "Philos', I think, and Froure's. Let them be together—they've earned it. Let them live at the edge of Ledom—they're used to it. And let the young humans know only them, and remember us; and then let their children and their children's children remember them and make of us a myth . . .

"And let us always watch them, perhaps help them by accidents and bits of luck; if they don't succeed they will fail and if they fail they will die, as humanity has died before . . .

"And one day, some other way, we will start humanity again, or perhaps meet humanity again . . . but somehow, some day (when we know ourselves well) we can be sure, and then Ledom will cease, and humanity will begin at last."

On a starry night Philos and Froure sat outside for a few minutes in the thin cold air. Quesbu and Soutin had left an hour before, after a real family dinner, and had gone back to their snug log-and-sod house out on the wooded mesa.

"Froure . . . ?"

"What is it?"

"The youngsters . . ."

"I know," said Froure. "It's hard to put your finger on it . . . but there's something wrong."

"Not a big something . . . maybe it's just pregnancy."

"Maybe . . ."

From the star-silvered dark: "Philos . . . ?"

"Quesbu! What on earth . . . did you forget something?"

He came out of the shadows, walking slowly, his head down. "I wanted to . . . Philos?"

"Yes, child; I'm here."

"Philos, Sou is . . . well, she's unhappy."

"Whatever's wrong?"

"I . . ." Suddenly he flung his head up, and in the dim glow of his face, stars stood: tears. "Sou's so wonderful but . . . but all the time I love somebody called Laura and I can't help it!" he burst out.

Philos put an arm around his shoulders and laughed; but laughed so softly, with such compassion, that it was a stroking. "Ah, that's not your Laura, that's Charlie's!" he crooned. "Charlie's dead now, Ques."

Froure said, "Remember the loving, Quesbu; but yes—forget Laura."

Quesbu said, "But he loved her so much. . . ."

"Froure's right," said Philos. "He loved her. Use the love. It's bigger than Charlie—it's still alive. Take it back and give it to Sou."

Suddenly—Philos thought it was a glory in his face, but it was the sky—suddenly the sky blazed; the stars were gone. Froure cried out. And their familiar mesa was unfamiliar in the silver overcast of a Ledom sky.

"So it comes; at last it comes," said Philos. He felt very sad. "I wonder when Seace will be able to take it down again . . . Ques, run back to Soutin—quick! Tell her it's all right; the silver sky is keeping us safe."

Quesbu sprinted away. Froure called, "Tell her you love her!"

Quesbu turned without breaking stride, waved just like Charlie Johns, and was gone through the woods.

Froure sighed, and laughed a little, too.

Philos said, "I don't think I'll tell him . . . the love's too good to spoil . . . poor Charlie. His Laura married someone else, you know."

"I didn't know!"

"Yes—you know perfectly well you can cut off a cerebrostyle recording at any point. Seace and Mielwis just naturally cut off Charlie's record at a point where he was full of love; he might understand Ledom a bit better. But actually Charlie had a bit more memory than that."

"He was in that flying thing because he wanted to get away from—"

" 'Fraid not. He just got tired of her, which is why she married someone else. But that I wouldn't tell Quesbu."

"Oh, please don't," said Froure.

"At loving . . . amateurs," chuckled Philos. "Actually, Charlie was in that plane being flown to a place on the coast not too far from here. They had some bad earthquakes down there that year, and he was a bulldozer operator, you know. *Oh!*" he cried, looking up.

The sky began to shimmer, then to sparkle.

"Oh, pretty!" cried Froure.

"Fallout," said Philos. "They're at it again, the idiots."

They began to wait.

POSTSCRIPT

You homo saps. are funny people. I just read some figures wherein a large group of my fellow-citizens were asked if they thought all men were equal, and 61% said Yes. The same people were then asked if Negoes were equal to whites and with the very next breath 4% said Yes—and this without the sound of a shifting gear. To illustrate further: I once wrote a fairly vivid story about a man being unfaithful to his wife and no one made any scandalous remarks about me. I then wrote a specific kind of narrative about a woman being unfaithful to her husband and nobody had anything scandalous to say about my wife. *But* I wrote an empathetic sort of tale about some homosexuals and my mailbox filled up with cards drenched with scent and letters written in purple ink with green capitals. As good Philos says herein: *you* cannot be objective about sex, especially when it's outside certain parameters. Hence this disclaimer, friend: keep your troubles to yourself. I wear no siken sporran.

It was my aim in writing *Venus Plus X a)* to write a decent book *b)* about sex. It is impossible to attempt such a thing without touching upon religion, which is impossible to do without touching rather heavily upon some of your toes. If this hurts, I am sorry about the pain. My own toes stand firmly upon two planks in the

Bill of Rights, and if you have a book which refutes me, I promise that I shall read it with full attention and that *I will not burn it*.

Finally, I'd like your help in stacking these books spread all over my desk, partly because some of them are heavy and partly because it really might interest you to know whereout some of the *Venus Plus X* material was dredged. (Almost.) Needless to say, I make no claim to having transferred the contents of any of these books *in toto* into my manuscript. But they are, one and all, provocative tomes, and I list them for provocation's sweet sake; and where due and acceptable, to extend my thanks to the authors.

Holy Bible: Oxford Concordance. *The Human Body and How It Works*, by Elbert Tokay, Ph. D., Signet (NAL). *The Transients*, four parts, by Wm. H. Whyte Jr., *Fortune* magazine, 1953. *The Varieties of Religious Experience* by William James, Modern Library (Random House). Cunningham's *Manual of Practical Anatomy*, Oxford Medical Pubs., 1937. *Patterns of Culture*, Ruth Benedict, Mentor, 1953. *The Disappearance*, especially Chapter 13, p. 262, by Philip Wylie, Pocket Books edition, 1958. *Psychoanalysis and Religion* by Erich Fromm, Yale University Press, 1950. Various recent magazine articles by Margaret Mead. *Sex in History*, by G. Rattray Taylor, Ballantine, 1960, and *Are Clothes Modern?* by Bernard Rudofsky, Theobald, 1947. (These last two are among the most startling, informative, and thought-provoking books you could pick up.) Most of the Ledom names came from an article by John R. Pierce (J. J. Coupling), "Science for Art's Sake," in *Astounding Science Fiction* for November 1950, in listings of "words" constructed by the use of a table of probabilities and a table of random numbers. "Ledom" itself comes from a can of my favorite tobacco spelled backwards. All original trade names and advertising slogans herein copyrighted herewith.

NEW YORK
June 1960

FINE SCIENCE FICTION AND
FANTASY TITLES AVAILABLE
FROM CARROLL & GRAF

☐ Ballard, J.G./THE DROWNED WORLD	$3.95
☐ Ballard, J.G./THE TERMINAL BEACH	$3.50
☐ Dick, Philip K./TIME OUT OF JOINT	$3.95
☐ Disch, Thomas M./334	$3.95
☐ Hodgson, William H./THE HOUSE ON THE BORDERLAND	$3.50
☐ Moorcock, Michael/BEHOLD THE MAN	$2.95
☐ Moorcock, Michael/FANTASY: THE 100 BEST BOOKS	$15.95
☐ Mundy, Talbot/KING OF THE KHYBER RIFLES	$3.95
☐ Mundy, Talbot/OM, THE SECRET OF AHBOR VALLEY	$3.95
☐ Pringle, David/SCIENCE FICTION: THE 100 BEST NOVELS	$7.95
☐ Siodmak, Curt/DONOVAN'S BRAIN	$3.50
☐ Sladek, John/RODERICK	$3.95
☐ Sladek, John/RODERICK AT RANDOM	$3.95
☐ Stevens, Francis/CITADEL OF FEAR	$3.50
☐ Stevens, Francis/CLAIMED	$3.50
☐ Stevens, Francis/THE HEADS OF CERBERUS	$3.50
☐ Sturgeon, Theodore/THE DREAMING JEWELS	$3.95
☐ Wolfe, Bernard/LIMBO	$4.95

Available from fine bookstores everywhere or use this coupon for ordering:

Carroll & Graf Publishers, Inc., 260 Fifth Avenue, N.Y., N.Y. 10001

Please send me the books I have checked above. I am enclosing $_____ (please add $1.75 per title to cover postage and handling.) Send check or money order—no cash or C.O.D.'s please. N.Y. residents please add 8¼% sales tax.

Mr/Mrs/Miss _____

Address _____

City _____ State/Zip _____

Please allow four to six weeks for delivery.

MORE EROTIC CLASSICS FROM CARROLL & GRAF

☐ Anonymous/ALTAR OF VENUS $3.95
☐ Anonymous/AUTOBIOGRAPHY OF A FLEA $3.95
☐ Anonymous/CONFESSIONS OF AN ENGLISH
    MAID $3.95
☐ Anonymous/FANNY HILL'S DAUGHTER $3.95
☐ Anonymous/MADELEINE $3.95
☐ Anonymous/A MAID'S JOURNEY $3.95
☐ Anonymous/THE MEMOIRS OF JOSEPHINE $3.95
☐ Anonymous/MICHELE $3.95
☐ Anonymous/CONFESSIONS OF EVELINE $3.95
☐ Anonymous/VENUS IN INDIA $3.95
☐ Anonymous/SECRET LIVES $3.95
☐ Anonymous/THREE TIMES A WOMAN $3.95
☐ Anonymous/VENUS REMEMBERED $3.95
☐ van Heller, Marcus/HOUSE OF BORGIA $3.95
☐ van Heller, Marcus/THE LOINS OF AMON $3.95
☐ Villefranche, Anne-Marie/FOLIES D'AMOUR $3.95
☐ Villefranche, Anne-Marie/PLAISIR D'AMOUR $3.95
☐ Von Falkensee, Margarete/BLUE ANGEL
    NIGHTS $3.95

Available from fine bookstores everywhere or use this coupon for ordering:

Carroll & Graf Publishers, Inc., 260 Fifth Avenue, N.Y., N.Y. 10001

Please send me the books I have checked above. I am enclosing $_____ (please add $1.75 per title to cover postage and handling.) Send check or money order—no cash or C.O.D.'s please. N.Y. residents please add 8¼% sales tax.

Mr/Mrs/Miss _____

Address _____

City _____ State/Zip _____

Please allow four to six weeks for delivery.

FINE WORKS OF FICTION AND NON-FICTION AVAILABLE FROM CARROLL & GRAF

- [ ] Asch, Sholem/EAST RIVER $3.95
- [ ] Brown, Harry/A WALK IN THE SUN $3.95
- [ ] Chester, Alfred/THE EXQUISITE CORPSE $4.95
- [ ] Burnett, W. R./HIGH SIERRA $3.50
- [ ] Cozzens, James Gould/THE LAST ADAM $4.95
- [ ] Crichton, Robert/THE CAMERONS $4.95
- [ ] Crichton, Robert/THE SECRET OF SANTA VITTORIA $3.95
- [ ] De Quincey, Thomas/CONFESSIONS OF AN ENGLISH OPIUM EATER AND OTHER WRITINGS $4.95
- [ ] Farrell, J.G./TROUBLES $4.95
- [ ] Farrell, J.G./THE SIEGE OF KRISHNAPUR $4.95
- [ ] Farrell, J.G./THE SINGAPORE GRIP $4.95
- [ ] Garbus, Martin/READY FOR THE DEFENSE $4.95
- [ ] Gresham, William Lindsay/NIGHTMARE ALLEY $3.50
- [ ] Gurney, Jr., A.R./THE SNOW BALL $4.50
- [ ] Higgins, George V./A CHOICE OF ENEMIES $3.50
- [ ] Higgins, George V./COGAN'S TRADE $3.50
- [ ] Higgins, George V./PENANCE FOR JERRY KENNEDY $3.50
- [ ] Hilton, James/RANDOM HARVEST $4.50
- [ ] Huxley, Aldous/GREY EMINENCE $4.95
- [ ] Innes, Hammond/THE NAKED LAND $3.50
- [ ] Innes, Hammond/ATLANTIC FURY $3.50
- [ ] Innes, Hammond/SOLOMON'S SEAL $3.50
- [ ] Innes, Hammond/THE WRECK OF THE MARY DEARE $3.50
- [ ] Johnson, Josephine/NOW IN NOVEMBER $4.50
- [ ] Kipling, Rudyard/THE LIGHT THAT FAILED $3.95
- [ ] L'Amour, Louis/LAW OF THE DESERT BORN $2.95
- [ ] Lewis, Norman/THE SICILIAN SPECIALIST $3.50

☐	Lewis, Norman/THE MAN IN THE MIDDLE	$3.50
☐	Mason, A.E.W./THE FOUR FEATHERS	$3.95
☐	Martin, David/FINAL HARBOR	$4.95
☐	Masters, John/THEOPHILUS NORTH	$4.95
☐	Masters, John/BHOWANI JUNCTION	$4.50
☐	Mitford, Nancy/PIGEON PIE	$3.95
☐	Mitford, Nancy/CHRISTMAS PUDDING	$3.95
☐	O'Hara, John/FROM THE TERRACE	$4.95
☐	O'Hara, John/SERMONS AND SODA WATER	$4.95
☐	O'Hara, John/HOPE OF HEAVEN	$3.95
☐	O'Hara, John/A RAGE TO LIVE	$4.95
☐	O'Hara, John/TEN NORTH FREDERICK	$4.50
☐	Proffitt, Nicholas/GARDENS OF STONE	$4.50
☐	Purdy, James/CABOT WRIGHT BEGINS	$4.50
☐	Rechy, John/BODIES AND SOULS	$4.50
☐	Reilly, Sidney/BRITAIN'S GREATEST SPY	$3.95
☐	Scott, Paul/THE LOVE PAVILION	$4.50
☐	Scott, Paul/THE CORRIDA AT SAN FELIU	$3.95
☐	Scott, Paul/A MALE CHILD	$3.95
☐	Short, Luke/MARSHAL OF VENGEANCE	$2.95
☐	Smith, Joseph/THE DAY THE MUSIC DIED	$4.95
☐	Taylor, Peter/IN THE MIRO DISTRICT	$3.95
☐	Thirkell, Angela/THE BRANDONS	$4.95
☐	Thirkell, Angela/POMFRET TOWERS	$4.95
☐	Wharton, William/SCUMBLER	$3.95
☐	Wilder, Thornton/THE EIGTH DAY	$4.95
☐	Wilder, Thornton/THE CABALA	$3.95

Available from fine bookstores everywhere or use this coupon for ordering:

Carroll & Graf Publishers, Inc., 260 Fifth Avenue, N.Y., N.Y. 10001

Please send me the books I have checked above. I am enclosing $_____ (please add $1.75 per title to cover postage and handling.) Send check or money order—no cash or C.O.D.'s please. N.Y. residents please add 8¼% sales tax.

Mr/Mrs/Miss _____

Address _____

City _____ State/Zip _____

Please allow four to six weeks for delivery.